Congo Spider Fangs

Treasure Rebels, Volume 2

Gerard Doris

Published by Gerard Doris, 2023.

This is a work of fiction. Similarities to real people, places, or events are entirely coincidental.

CONGO SPIDER FANGS

First edition. September 28, 2023.

Copyright © 2023 Gerard Doris.

ISBN: 979-8223594574

Written by Gerard Doris.

Also by Gerard Doris

Treasure Rebels
Nile River Scorpion
Congo Spider Fangs
Amazon Swamp Victory
India Yeti Pirates
Greek Gladiator Sharks

Standalone
Wrath of the Renegades

Watch for more at https://www.adventurefictionforever.com.

Table of Contents

PROLOGUE 1
PART I: CONGO RAINFOREST 15
PART II: THE "DOCTOR" 29
PART III: SPIDER HELICOPTER 55
EPILOGUE 85

PROLOGUE

(Central Africa – Congo River)

The brutally fierce howl of an African leopard echoed from deep within the Congo Jungle. The medical team huddled inside a large reinforced tent beside the flowing waters of the Congo River didn't even bother to look up. They were too busy loading three secured carbon fibre transport containers, each the size of a suitcase, with emergency medical supplies.

All three middle aged doctors worked as quickly as possible because every minute counted. With the task almost complete, the only woman of the group went over to a small laminated fridge and hurriedly but carefully opened the small aluminum door. A cloud of white frozen air which looked like steam whooshed out in every direction as she put her gloved hand inside the fridge and pulled out a small carton which contained six orange vials.

Each vial was wrapped in orange plastic with the label ANTI-VENOM printed on the outside. Uneasily and with fingers trembling she lowered three vials into two of the cases, taping them securely into a special velvet compartment. Inside each of the two cases were also rows of empty medical needles.

The third case was labelled SPECIMEN on the outside and enclosed a plastic medical bag which containing the remains of an unidentified creature. Now that the vials were secure the lead doctor who was also the tallest by far stepped forward and carefully locked the three lids into place by typing onto a number pad imbedded in the containers handles. The three containers beeped as the locks were set in place, and a visible digital timer next to each keypad began counting down from 24:00 hrs.

He then looked at his watch and sighed in relief, "Five minutes to helicopter withdrawal." Each doctor then picked up one of the cases and hurriedly rushed out into the African daylight.

Thirty feet to their left they were greeted by the deafening roar of the mighty Congo River as torrents of water splashed up onto the grassy bank. Flowing through the Congo jungle and much of Africa's centre, the Congo River is one of the longest rivers in the world and the deepest...at a depth of more than seven hundred feet!

The doctors rushed across the wet grass towards a much larger tent guarded by two Congolese men wearing suits which concealed their loaded firearms. Behind the tent two Jeeps and two pickup trucks idled in the hot sun, while beyond them a great twin rotor Chinook transport helicopter sat prepared for take-off.

As they approached two soldiers opened the tent canvas for them to walk through, no questions asked. Once inside the tent they saw two men wearing pilot uniforms studying a large map strewn across the single desk. To their left stood businessman and humanitarian Mr. John Jabari, a seven foot tall native of Central Africa, wearing a black business suit and nervously rubbing his eyes as he spoke into a satellite radio receiver. He waited patiently for a reply but meaningless screeching static was all that came from the speakers.

He replaced the receiver in frustration and shook hands with the doctors, addressing the lead medic who was as tall as he was.

"Dr. Fleming, thank you, each of you. The medicine is ready?"

Dr. Fleming nodded his head "yes" then pointed at the pilots.

"I understand we have a few minutes before they take off?"

Mr. Jabari shook his head and replied, "No, only moments. We just received a call from the village that a storm is coming from the East. No time to wait. They leave the moment you put those cases on the helo."

Dr. Fleming nodded toward his equals saying, "In that case Mr. Jabari, my colleagues here Dr. Smith and Dr. Gibson wish to thank you for the opportunity to-"

Mr. Jabari lifted his hand and interrupted the Doctor.

"It is my people who want to thank you. On behalf of the village which I represent, I cannot thank each of you enough for helping to save their lives. I will see to it that your home countries in Europe and yours Dr. Smith in Egypt are well aware that the three of you have saved many lives."

The doctors humbly thanked him then laid the three cases onto the table before the two pilots. Without a word the pilots picked them up and headed for the exit, the younger pilot carrying two of the three cases.

But before they disappeared outside Dr. Fleming quickly called out to them, "The anti-venom must be used as soon as you land! The cases are pressurized and specially sealed to keep the vials cold. But only for 24 hours. Once the cases lose their pressure the medicine will warm up and become useless. The specimen also needs to remain preserved as well for further study."

The older of the two pilots didn't even bother to acknowledge the Doctor but instead kept moving and disappeared past the tent curtain, already thinking of the flight-plan. The younger pilot in his early thirties whose nametag read TERENCE JABARI, instead nodded his head in understanding and replied to Fleming in a deep accent, "We understand Doctor. We will get the medicine up the river in no time. We are the best there is at flying transport helicopters."

He then stepped through the canvas and out into the African daylight. He was followed behind by the doctors and Jabari who walked past him and the Chinook towards the idling jeeps.

Both pilots walked up the open cargo bay door and secured the three cases in the expansive hold. Without a word they then walked through the compartment up to the cockpit, quickly strapping themselves into the bucket seats and hitting the button to close the door. Gradually the immense door lifted off the ground until it locked in place, while the twin motor blades began to spin fiercely and the engine roared.

Showtime.

Through the cockpit glass they could see Jabari and the doctors tying their seatbelts, while Jabari's five man security team dismantled the two specialized tents in under forty seconds. The two tents, medical equipment, tables and chairs were loaded onto the back of the pickup trucks, and in seconds every man had jumped aboard or onto a jeep for the ride back. With a wave of his hand Jabari signalled the pilots to leave and the Chinook began to rise toward the sky.

But at that moment a strange figure stepped out onto the clearing directly in front of the vehicles, waving his hands for everyone to stop. Jabari leaned out of the jeep and stared at the man puzzled. The man in the clearing yelled something to the businessman while pointing at the helicopter.

Jabari looked up at the Chinook twenty feet off the ground and signalled Terence to land. In seconds Terence had the helo back on the ground, the engines still roaring while he and the older pilot waited and watched impatiently, refusing to completely shut down the engines.

Jabari opened the driver's side door and stepped down to speak with the stranger. Instinctively his men jumped onto the grass as well and protectively circled him, weapons ever ready. Jabari nodded to his men and told them to lower their guns, but he didn't tell them to back away either. His men understood the message and watched.

Jabari looked at the mysterious man wearing a long full length black raincoat. He was in his early thirties, had a completely bald head, long blond goatee, and light blue eyes that almost looked colourless. Unlike most men, he was tall enough to look Jabari straight in the eye. Jabari looked straight back, recognizing the man.

"Doctor McClory, I understood you were still in the Sudan helping with the food aid. I didn't think you were planning to go into the rainforest here in the Congo for another week."

McClory smiled and pointed to the edge of the rainforest, where three more men also wearing the same black rain coats stepped out into the clearing and approached the jeep, carrying an old crate that looked a hundred years old.

"My men and I were no longer needed in the Sudan, so we were approved to enter the Congo ahead of time for our research. We sailed up the river and went ashore four miles from here. Our boat sank a couple hours ago. By God's grace we heard your vehicles and helicopter. I came running while they carried our gear."

Jabari was not a fool. He looked at the hundred year old crate which was missing a few boards and had been taped over to cover the holes. He replied disconcerted, "Your gear? What exactly was the nature of your expedition?"

McClory grinned innocently and replied in his strange accent, "We are botanists from Greece Mr. Jabari, looking to discover, study, and collect unidentified fauna. Most of our equipment went under with the boat. But we saved enough to still carry out our scientific expedition. We stumbled upon an immense supply of previously unidentified plants! We accomplished what we came here for! Our discoveries along with our equipment is in the crate, which was supplied to us by a kind farmer upriver."

McClory then pointed at the helicopter while saying, "With your permission we will fly to the fishermen's village with the crate, the medical team there will have the equipment needed to properly prepare our discoveries for the long trip up north to Europe."

Jabari replied bluntly, "Dr. McClory, that helicopter is delivering newly created medicine to save over fifty dying Congolese at that village, the doctor there has his hands full already. Load your men and the crate onto this Jeep instead, we will be back at my headquarters in four hours and you can take care of everything there."

Jabari then pointed to Dr. Fleming who was sitting in the passenger seat. "I have my own medical team with me. They treat people, not plants, but I'm sure they will help you the moment we arrive at headquarters."

Dr. McClory looked horrified and after a moment's hesitation replied, "How long will it take the helicopter to get to the village?"

"Under two hours. The village is located right along this mighty river."

"The specimens will be ruined in this heat after three hours. They must be taken to the village instead with us aboard."

Jabari had had enough. He didn't care about botany or pleasing this creepy scientist. All he cared about was that two of Africa's best pilots leave immediately and deliver the newly created anti-venom. But he knew that if Dr. McClory complained later, his own business ties with local government, which was already strained, may be over. He quickly decided.

"Doctor, load your medicine on the helicopter, but you and your team come with me. I'll radio to the village that your crate be protected and preserved, and that no one is to open or go near it. After you've spoken with my superiors you can then fly out to the village immediately sometime tomorrow."

McClory prepared to protest but Jabari was already ordering his men to take the crate. McClory's men began to protest fiercely, but gave up when it became clear Jabari's armed men paid them no attention.

As three of Jabari's men disappeared inside the helicopter with the wooden crate, McClory tried to ease the tension and smoothly said to Jabari, "Thank you for accommodating us. Your people have been very kind to my team. We are very lucky to even be here in Africa! I know we are the only ones who have been approved for jungle expeditions here in the Congo for quite some time."

Jabari's three men reappeared, signalled their boss that the crate was properly secured, and hopped onto the nearest Jeep. As they did so the Chinook immediately re-closed the cargo bay door then soared free of the ground and headed directly upriver, seventy feet above the roaring river water towards the fishermen's village.

Jabari stepped back into his own Jeep and closed the door. "Actually your team is the second. There are treasure hunters in the area. My government approved them two weeks ago."

McClory looked up and a surprised and intrigued look crossed his face. "Treasure hunters Mr. Jabari? What are they...looking for?"

Jabari was tired of talking and instead pointed to the Jeep's back. "You and your fellow botanists get in and hold on...my men never, ever, slow down."

Twenty minutes later the Chinook continued soaring across the African sky, following the Congo River which twisted through the almost haunted looking and impenetrably dense rainforest. Far in the distance storm clouds could be seen, but for now the weather was flawless, and the searing hot sunlight glistened off the helicopter's fuselage.

"I'd say we have a couple hours before the storm hits us."

The older pilot, whom everyone simply called David, adjusted the controls and as the chopper picked up even more speed he replied, "I'm going to make sure we're there in under fifty min."

The minutes passed, and after looking back at the cargo compartment Terence undid the bucket seat belts and said, "I want to double check the medicine."

David didn't even look up as he simply responded, "Roger."

Terence stepped past the bucket seats into the lengthy cargo compartment which was wide enough for a car to drive through. But with the three cases and strange looking crate lined up along the sides, he only had a few feet of walking space through the centre.

He examined the straps to ensure they were still tight, an unnecessary formality with David or him at the controls. The helo hadn't even dipped or shaken enough to spill a cup of coffee in the last half hour, while Terence's take off had been picture perfect.

He then looked at each case timer, smiling for the first time in hours, honoured and happy he had been given the opportunity to deliver the medicine and help save lives.

Suddenly the helicopter lurched and the tattered wooden crate belonging to the botanists slid against his leg. He looked up in surprise and pushed the crate back against the wall and retightened the suddenly slackened strap. He looked up and spoke through his headset intercom.

"What was that?"

David responded calmly, "What do you mean? Nothing happened."

"The quick bank to the left."

"We've been flying straight for ten minutes."

Terence uneasily double checked the strap to make sure it would hold and after sitting back down into the cockpit he said as he buckled himself in, "The old crate broke free and I had to retighten it. If you didn't move then the crate's weight must have caused it to come loose. Must weigh over a hundred pounds! My Uncle's men must not have known what they were doing when they tied it in."

"What did Jabari say over the intercom before we left...that it was filled with plants?"

"And botanist *equipment*."

Both pilots looked at each and David replied sombrely, "I don't care what Jabari said, let's have the doctor in the village run it through that x-ray machine. I don't want to risk leaving drugs or illegal weapons there."

Terence looked out at the storm still three miles away in the distant sky. "No complaint from me."

Another minute passed and David pointed ahead. "See those series of waterfalls a half mile up ahead?"

"Yeah?"

"Once we pass over them we'll start flying over the rapids, and then the village is only ten minutes away."

"Copy that."

Suddenly the helicopter shook, as if a gale of wind had briefly brushed against the helo's side. Both pilots looked at one another then looked back.

The crate had broken free of the yellow strap once again, and this time the crate's lid had popped open as well.

Terence stood up but froze at what he saw.

Without turning his eyes away from the view ahead David asked anxiously, "What's wrong!?"

"The crate moved."

"I know that!"

"On its own."

"What??"

Suddenly the crate toppled completely over and Terence saw the spiders.

Nine hairy arachnids each the size of a large dinner plate, with strange black and purple lines across their bodies, crawled out of the crate and quickly began to hop onto the steel cases and crawl up the cargo compartment's ribbed sides, ceiling, and everywhere else.

"Close the cockpit door!"

Before Terence could react one of the creatures jumped five feet through the air and landed directly onto the back of David's leather chair.

"Get the thing off!"

But before Terence could move the spider bit through the chair and David yelled in pain as the two inch fangs easily sliced through the chair and into his back.

Acting on instinct Terence reached forward and grabbed the purple haired spider, throwing it as hard as possible back into the compartment where it smashed against one of the medicine cases and dropped onto the metal floor squirming and stunned.

Terence slammed the door and for half a minute David assured Terence he felt fine, until suddenly he began coughing and blood appeared out of his nose. Terence reached to help but before he could two more spiders that had crawled inside unseen before the cockpit door closed jumped up and onto the control panel.

Then everything flew in every direction as the helicopter began spinning and losing altitude.

Terence picked himself up and reached forward for the control stick wondering what had happened. Then he looked and saw David was motionless and no longer in control.

With the helicopter still spinning and dropping Terence barely held on, and after climbing back into his seat regained almost full control...until one of the spiders jumped straight onto his face.

He instinctively reached up and swatted the arachnid away, doing everything in his power to keep control of the helo at the same time. But when he looked up he knew he wouldn't prevent the crash in time.

Through the cockpit window all he could see was open sky, then the very top of one of the waterfalls as the helicopter dropped and crashed directly into it.

A sharp horrific screech filled the cabin as the chopper's right side was breached by a sharp jagged stone, protruding a full foot into the Chinook's cargo hold.

Water began to pour in and Terence opened his eyes to see his right shoulder was covered in blood, and the entire helicopter was resting at a 45 degree angle. He crawled across the damaged instruments and shattered glass to check his friend's pulse who sat lifeless.

He then punched the control panel in rage.

David was gone.

Terence then opened the cockpit door and looked through the cargo compartment. Water was pouring in rapidly through the breach, and to his surprise the spiders didn't crawl away but *towards* the growing pool of water.

He quickly realized what had happened. The helicopter had smashed onto one of the sharp outcroppings of stone lining the rim of the waterfall, and because of the choppers sheer weight, force of the crash, and immense size of the sharp stone, the helo was now pinned to the very top of the waterfall. Shocked he further realized that half of the chopper was now hanging over the edge of the waterfall out into open space.

He looked at the radio. Broken.

He then looked down at the cargo in fear.

Could he save the medicine?

He could see the spiders were crawling atop the medicine cases that were still tied securely to the wall opposite the stone breach.

Could he run forward and grasp one of the cases without getting bitten?

He didn't have a choice. The fishermen in the village were doomed if he didn't save some of it.

He stepped forward and approached the closest case, hearing the helo groan in protest with every step he took forward. With the tear in the Chinook's fuselage, including the endless pounding it was taking from the surging water all around it, he guessed it could topple over the falls at any moment.

He covered his hand with his jacket sleeve and aggressively pushed one of the spiders off the case. It fell into the rising pool of water on the floor and didn't resurface.

He quickly undid the strap holding the three cases in place and lifted one of them. He stepped back and cautiously walked towards the cockpit by stepping over another spider that had suddenly dropped down from above in front of him. He reached the cockpit and not seeing any spiders inside he quickly locked the cockpit door, hoping there weren't any hidden from view. He then grasped the case and tried opening the digital lock, wanting to pull out the vials of medicine because he would never be able to swim with the cumbersome case.

Nothing worked.

He then opened the pilot's door and looked down in terror at the sixty foot drop. He wondered about the likelihood of whirlpools at the bottom of the falls, or how strong the river current was. Suddenly he froze as a strange sound met his ears.

He looked up at the strange sound of hissing and saw three of the arachnids slowly approaching as they crawled atop the underside of the cockpit roof... towards his head.

He knew what he had to do. He would have to hope the helicopter would remain pinned to the falls. And he would have to hope he could reach Jabari before the timers ran out on the cases.

He leaned forward and kicking the cockpit door back open slid the case back into the cargo hold. Then just before the spiders reached his head he jumped through the open door and disappeared into the roaring water, his descent completely concealed by the jungle mist which hung over the falls.

PART I: CONGO RAINFOREST

(Two hours later – Congo Jungle – 10 miles from John Jabari's home)

"Two bloody weeks here in this green oven! I almost miss the Egypt desert."

Amber Monette grinned and looked at one of her two best friends, Travis Jagson. "Travis, to be fair the temperature was actually four degrees hotter when we left Egypt."

The former boxer took a long drink and spit the last mouthful of lukewarm water out. "I miss home. The breeze, the beach girls, the sunsets, the-"

"Hawaii has hot jungles too!"

Travis laughed and opening a new canteen of water replied jokingly, "Trust me, my Hawaiian jungles feel air conditioned compared to here."

Amber just shook her head and gave up, knowing she would never win any discussion that involved his home state. She turned back to the old notebook in her hand and continued studying its tattered and strange pages. After reading for a minute she closed the book and said, "Wolfgang was such a sick eccentric. Everything he wrote was vague, nothing clear or straightforward. Very un-German like."

Travis put the canteen away and slid the silver coloured machete out of its sheath behind his back to continue the journey forward.

"Are we sure the waterfall still exists? Wolfgang and his buddy were searching here back in the thirties. Maybe the jungle swallowed it, or the Congo River changed enough that-"

Amber shrugged her shoulders.

"Maddox doesn't think so. Remember the jungle drawings on page 47? Almost picture perfect of the Congo River's topography near here. If the River hasn't changed in this part of the jungle in the last eighty some years, Maddox is sure the waterfall must still be preserved as well. Wolfgang's words were horribly cryptic, but his drawings bordered on art and were precise to a fault."

Travis began slashing away to clear a path and replied, "Yeah, but putting aside his artistic geography skills for a moment, you're forgetting he also drew a bunch of weird animals he claimed the Bounty Hunter caught for food while they traveled through here, and don't forget the weird insects and cave creatures."

Amber put the notebook away in her backpack and sighed in agreement, "I didn't forget. I'm still trying to forget that bat he drew with the extra set of ears and teeth."

As they continued walking forward she pulled out a handheld satellite radio and pushed the call button.

"Maddox, do you read me? We're approaching the hill."

Static.

She tried again.

"Maddox! We're approaching the hill!"

This time she heard him respond, but not through the radio.

"Waterfall found!"

She and Travis looked up to see their friend standing twenty feet above them at the crest of a small jungle hill.

Maddox Tarver was the leader of their group. He was in his late twenties, of average height, a natural athlete, and everywhere he went he carried the relaxed and confident manner of one who never panicked no matter the situation. Two years previous he had recruited both Travis and Amber to join him in traveling the globe. In that time they had discovered over eight million dollars worth of treasure on three continents. Their discoveries became the stuff of legend, and soon news media around the world gave them the title "Treasure Rebels" because of their unorthodox methods for finding treasure. He grinned beneath the unusual copper sunglasses he almost never took off, and looked down at his two best friends.

"You won't believe where it is!"

Amber smiled and put the notebook away, calling up to him, "Okay...wait for us!"

With her natural shoulder length red hair, incredible smile, and beautiful physique many men made the mistake of thinking Amber was a model. In reality she had studied astrophysics in university, after which she was hired by NASA and became a top expert in space travel to Mars. But despite only being in her mid-twenties, she gave up her promising career to join Maddox and Travis. The media were perplexed, but all she would say was that she wanted "to search the beautiful world for unspeakable buried treasure."

Beside her Travis Jagson had also jumped at the chance to join Maddox, walking away from a perfect 40-0 boxing record and the likely opportunity to fight in a heavyweight title bout. Despite "retiring" he still maintained his 250 all muscle frame, and at almost six foot six was one of the largest and most physically fit men on earth. Because he was roughly the same age as Maddox and Amber, sports journalists demanded to know why someone who still had prime boxing years left would give it up. He would simply smile and reply, "No comment."

Because of their age, some in the media considered them to be little more than adrenaline junkies who had gotten lucky a couple times stumbling upon treasure. The media couldn't have been more wrong, or even guessed at the seriousness of the Treasure Rebels true reasons for travelling the globe.

All three were dressed for extensive jungle exploration, and each one carried tranquilizer guns and machetes for safety, along with backpacks full of specialized equipment for navigation, communication, medicine, and tools.

After quickly hacking through the foliage they had climbed the hill and stood beside Maddox, whose usually spikey blond hair was now plastered flat atop his head due to the jungle humidity. Travis and Amber each pulled out a set of waterproof binoculars with blue lenses from their backpacks and studied the valley below.

At the bottom of the hill was a small lush valley filled with trees and large jungle plants which finally opened up into a large clearing, at the end of which stood a forty foot deep and fifteen foot wide waterfall. A slow moving shallow ravine fed by the waterfall snaked through the centre of the valley, before disappearing around a bend.

"Are you sure this is it?"

"I'm sure man."

They quickly rushed to the bottom of the hill, then carefully walked across a few stones to pass across the small ravine. They stopped and stood at the base of the falls, listening to the calm rhythm of the water endlessly cascading onto the rocks of the ravine.

Amber put away her binoculars and got out the notebook. "Maddox, it looks nothing like the drawing!"

Maddox grinned. "It looks exactly like it. He drew this ravine on page 28."

Amber began flipping through the notebook still not believing him. "I don't understand, are you certain? That's the section where he drew all the jungle plants and ravines, not the waterfalls."

Maddox walked away and stopped fifty feet from the falls, where he pulled out the machete and began hacking at a strange outcropping of vines and tree branches. After a moment he then tossed the machete blade into the soil and grasping the branches with both hands he pulled the entire mass to one side...revealing the opening to a strange cave, seven feet high by four feet wide, almost every inch covered in wet green grime.

Maddox grinned, the late afternoon sunlight reflecting off his copper sunglasses. "I'm certain."

==

They turned on their high powered LED flashlights and stepped to the dark edge of the cave's entrance, but waited to step inside. Amber then lifted a small computer tablet into the cave's entrance and tapped the screen a couple times. After three seconds it beeped twice. She nodded her head okay.

"No poisons in the air."

They stepped inside and walked forward sweeping the damp walls with their lights while Amber continued to monitor the tablet for signs of air trouble. As they continued forward they were surprised that the air was not only safe but surprisingly clean, almost refreshing. Also, the green mildew which had covered the cave's opening was now gone.

As they continued forward there was no sign of any insects or animals, only droplets of moisture on every inch of black rock. After twenty yards the cave twisted right, then left, then finally opened into a much larger cave, roughly diamond shaped and 3,000 square feet in total width. A hundred feet above them the jungle trees could be seen covering most of the opening above, preventing almost all of the sunlight from shining in.

Across from where they stood was the sought after waterfall, fifty feet in height, with water that appeared turquoise in colour due to the modest sunlight which illuminated it in the dark cave. Despite its height the water's current above was not too powerful, and the water did not pour over the edge with a roar but dropped quietly into the pool of water below.

As the water pooled at the base of the falls it fed a narrow ravine which flowed to the left towards a four foot wide crevice in the cave wall, where it then flowed out into the rainforest.

They stepped towards the falls.

Amber put away the tablet while saying, "When Wolfgang wrote that the medicine was behind the waterfall...I hoped it was just one of his lies and not real."

All three stepped onto the rocks below the falls, and then cautiously with the wall of turquoise water only inches away from their faces, they walked forward.

The water was freezing but shallow in depth. Their clothing was instantly drenched but they passed through the falling stream with one step. Now past they turned on their flashlights…to reveal a small rocky cavern completely empty except for a handful of broken pieces of wood from an old crate.

Stunned Maddox knelt down and examined each shattered piece. Without looking up he said, "The wood looks a hundred years old, but you can tell the crate was broken apart recently."

Amber picked up one of the boards and said, "We're the only ones to have read the notebook for seventy years. Wolfgang's grandson knows about the notebook, but even then we beat him to it."

Travis spit in disgust and said, "That creepy rat has been following us for over a year. I told you all I was afraid he and the others were getting close after the Mediterranean."

Amber threw the board down. "But we never saw one of them in Egypt."

"They could have been one of the ones on the river bank watching the yacht."

"Even so, if they did tail us, how did they find the cavern and why would they steal the medicine?"

Maddox slowly stood remaining quiet and panned his light across the entire cavern, including the bat infested ceiling. Despite their loud presence below not a single bat strayed from the rocky outcropping above. In fact, Maddox noticed that they seemed almost afraid to move, clinging close to one another as far from the ground as possible.

Maddox turned the light back towards the streaming water and without a word stepped back through the waterfall out into the main cave. His friends quickly followed. But as Amber stepped forward through the falling stream something dropped onto her shoulder then immediately fell into the pool of water and disappeared.

Back in the central cave with the others she quickly began scanning the ravine at the base of the falls with her light. "Did either of you see that?"

"See what?"

"Something dropped onto me as I walked through the falls. I never got a good look at it."

Before Maddox or Travis could reply an unusual hissing sound suddenly filled the cave, growing louder by the second. Immediately Amber and Travis's thoughts turned to Wolfgang's notebook and his frightening depictions of "cave creatures."

Maddox instead had already spotted the creature, and while it wasn't some mythical monster, it was horrifying.

"To the right! It's burrowing out of the ground!"

Travis and Amber spun to see a black red centipede, at least four feet long and two feet wide, crawl forward on its set of eighty small feet toward them, it's head and fangs shaking back and forth as it continued to screech in anger.

Travis was a man of action, but for the first time in his life he froze for a split second as the creature crawled towards him at an incredible speed. The centipede stopped and curled half its body upright, almost giving the appearance of a snake about to strike. Travis shook off the self-paralyses and dove to get out of the way while a dagger from Amber embedded in the centipede's side to no effect. Maddox then unloaded an entire chamber of tranquilizer darts into the creature's small face. But nothing stopped the centipede as it lunged forward onto Travis back and immediately began curling around his entire body like an Anaconda snake.

Travis was one of the strongest men on earth but he immediately knew he couldn't stop the choking power of the centipede from crushing his rib cage and lungs. He could already feel one of his ribs bending, about to break.

As Maddox and Amber rushed forward to free him he grabbed the creature's body with both arms and began trying vainly to push the creature away. The strange screeching grew in intensity and the centipede's small face curled upward above his head, the black four inch fangs hovering near his ear.

Travis gave up pushing and reaching forward he ripped Amber's dagger out of the centipede's side and drove the blade into the side of the creature's head, directly through both fangs. The centipede turned its head away and began shaking it violently to get rid of the blade, while Maddox and Amber tried to pull the centipede off of their friend.

Amber looked down and saw Travis's rifle in the soft dirt and realized it must have torn free as the centipede attacked. She rushed forward and pulled the rifle out of the dirt, but dropped the gun in fright as a purple coloured spider as large as her head crawled onto her hand, half of its body still grasping the rifle's barrel.

Instantly five more spiders roughly the same size, all also covered in purple furry hair, crawled out of the dirt in the same spot. But instead of attacking Amber they all rushed across the cave dirt and leaped onto the centipede's back, repeatedly biting through the red shell of the predatory arthropod.

The spiders continued biting and one of the hairy arachnids crawled furiously up the centipede's red shell until it stopped at the dagger blade which still pinned the centipede's jaws. The spider leaped onto the centipede's face and delivered the killer bite.

The screeching stopped and the centipede immediately crumpled lifeless to the dirt, and Travis leaped away as the spiders began eating.

Amber pulled the rifle out of the dirt, then she and Maddox each put an arm around their friend to support him. Together all three rushed through the cave and back out into the hot Congo jungle. They carefully walked across the stones and stopped on the other side of the ravine in the valley, where all three then dropped onto the pebbled dirt and mud to rest.

Travis mumbled a heartfelt thanks to his two friends and unbuttoned his safari shirt. Half his chest was covered by a sick looking bruise.

He splashed some water on the purple black bruise then drank the rest of the canteen in one mighty gulp. He spit out a mouthful of blood as he re-buttoned the shirt and nodded okay to the others.

"Just some bruised ribs. Still good y'all."

Amber disagreed. "No, not okay. You might-"

Travis put his hand up saying, "I'm know I'm good."

She turned to Maddox who was already looking down the ravine lost in thought.

"MADDOX! I know medical first aid. He's not okay."

Maddox looked up at her then at Travis who just continued smiling as he checked the rifle for any damage.

"He's okay."

"No he isn't! Guys, this isn't the time for either of you to play macho! I-"

Maddox suddenly sat up and pointed down the ravine to their right leading away from the valley. "You hear that?"

Amber and Travis paused but heard nothing.

"An African leopard" Maddox explained.

Travis cocked the rifle's chamber and climbing to his feet said, "I doubt it will head this way."

Maddox reloaded a new cartridge into the tranquilizer pistol and began jogging *towards* the howl. "That's why we're heading to it!"

"What?!?"

Without turning around Maddox kept moving forward and called back, "I also heard the sound of a man yelling."

Travis and Amber looked at one another and without another word followed Maddox.

After two minutes the leopard's howling grew louder, but whomever the man was that Maddox had heard yelling had stopped. After another minute of following ravine, the Treasure Rebels stopped and froze.

Ahead of them a giant African cat was dragging something across the ravine to the other bank. The six foot long jungle predator looked like a cheetah from a distance, but up close they could see the tell-tale shorter limbs, larger chest, and coat pattern which revealed it was indeed a leopard.

As they watched the leopard stopped and let go of its prey to look up at them. As it did so the "prey" rolled lifelessly forward in the shallow water, revealing the face and body of a man dressed in a military uniform.

Maddox aimed the pistol but knew the wild beast was out of range. He turned to Travis.

"Can you shoot it from here?"

Travis was already on one knee, looking at the giant cat through the rifle scope.

Maddox looked at the leopard then at Travis and continued, "Can you get it?"

Travis pulled the trigger and the dart silently imbedded into the leopard's neck, a perfect shot from forty yards.

"I got it."

They cautiously walked into the shallow ravine and approached the downed leopard. Once certain that a second shot was unnecessary they immediately pulled the man out of the water and laid him safely on the stony pebbled bank.

He was black, had a blood soaked right shoulder, and Maddox instantly recognized his ripped uniform as that of a helicopter pilot. The man slowly began to wake and Amber gave him a quick drink from one of their canteens. He continued drinking and then sat back against a large boulder exhausted, barely holding onto consciousness.

Behind them Travis had gone back to the leopard, carefully lifting the powerful creature up and onto his shoulders. He didn't want the jungle cat to drown in the ravine water, so he carried it to the other bank and gently laid the creature down in a safe spot, where in three hours he knew the leopard would awake.

In a haze the pilot noticed Travis and he jumped to his feet delirious, thinking that the leopard was still a danger. Amber and Maddox did their best to calm him down. He looked up into their faces but said nothing, seemingly too tired to even whisper, let alone speak. He slowly sat back down and watched still puzzled as Travis coolly walked back across the ravine while the leopard remained still on the other side.

Amber pulled out her satellite radio and punched in the number the Congo government had supplied for emergencies. Meanwhile Maddox continued to try to calm the pilot.

"Don't worry man, we got the leopard. You're good now."

The man looked up, his eyes full of delirious terror as he whispered:

"But what about the spiders?"

PART II: THE "DOCTOR"

(Three hours later – John Jabari's private estate)

The emergency helicopter touched down on the painted red X on the grassy field in front of John Jabari's private estate. The two story log home looked as if it had been built over a half century before, but the freshly painted porch and mahogany front door revealed it was still well kept up.

Beside Jabari's home was a small workshop, while behind the house was the guest's quarters, which currently was the home of his very small security force. Parked in front of the home was one of the jeeps that had escorted Jabari and the doctors, and sitting on a small bench and swing set was Jabari's wife and four children. Two guards sat asleep in the jeep while one stood sharply alert at the front door.

Before the white rotor blades had even begun to slow down Travis had opened the helo's main door and two medics jumped out onto the grass carrying Terence on a stretcher. Jabari appeared at the top step on the porch, where he waved the medics to bring Terence into the house. In moments the injured pilot had been carried inside.

A half minute later Jabari reappeared on the porch and pointed at the Treasure Rebels who were standing calmly beside the now quiet helicopter. "Come in please."

They followed Jabari into the house, surprised to see that the inside was sparsely filled with old and cheap furniture, the occasional used rug, and a kitchen that looked as if it belonged in a pioneer's homestead and not that of a modern businessman.

Jabari noticed their expressions and he said, "It is morally wrong for a man in my position to live richly while so many here in Africa have so little. As long as we're safe, have food, and a few toys for the children, my wife and I are happy to live here."

They then followed Jabari into a large dining room, complete with a large but scarred dinner table, wooden chairs, and an intricately carved fireplace that was the only source of heat or light at night.

A white cloth was laid across the dining room table and Terence was laid across it. Immediately the medics began replacing the bloody shoulder bandages they had applied during the helicopter ride with new ones.

The front door opened and Jabari's wife, an attractive woman of forty, quickly entered the dining room with a message for her husband. "The helicopter pilot says he must leave for town in a few moments, another emergency call where they're needed. But the doctors you contacted for help will arrive by car in moments."

He gave her a brief kiss on the forehead and said, "Thank you Jezebel. Could you take the little ones upstairs until Terence here is feeling better?"

"Of course. Will Terence be all right?"

"He's a Jabari, of course he will be."

As Jezebel left and closed the dining room door behind her, Amber pointed at Terence and said, "Is he your son as well?"

John went over to the window which overlooked the front porch and looking out expectantly he replied, "No, he's my nephew. One of the best helicopter pilots in all of Africa."

They heard a car pull up and Jabari turned away from the window, a look of relief across his usually stone-like face.

"The doctors are here."

He then turned and warmly shook hands with the two medics, thanking them for their successful rescue mission and telling them that they could now leave for their next call.

"Tell your pilot I am indebted to him as well."

"An honour as always Mr. Jabari to help you any way we can."

With that the medics picked up the empty stretcher and were gone.

Moments after they left the mansion the sound of heavy boots from the new visitors could be heard in the hallway, and the dining room door slowly swung open...

To reveal Dr. McClory and his fellow "botanists."

Jabari barked furiously, "Where is Dr. Fleming and the others?"

Dr. McClory gave his usual disturbing smirk and replied, "They are currently on a plane headed towards Egypt. We volunteered to replace them."

Jabari had already pulled out his smartphone and was rapidly dialling. He hit send and placing the phone against his ear responded indignantly, "We need a real doctor, not a group of botanists."

Jabari's call went through and in moments Dr. Fleming responded. In ten seconds the anti-venom expert had certified that Dr. McClory's story was true.

"But he studies plants! My nephew-"

Dr. Fleming replied, "McClory and his men are trained doctors from the U.S., I have their papers here. One of them was even an army medic. Botany is only a hobby for them. They said that their trip here to Africa was some sort of vacation."

Dr. Fleming suddenly paused for a second, before continuing with the hard truth. "I don't like McClory either. But we can't abandon our duties in Egypt at the moment. I'm sorry but they're your nephew's only hope, all their papers check out."

Jabari thanked him and ended the call. His instincts were incredibly sharp, and his instincts told him McClory and his men were crooked. But he knew his nephew would probably die without their help.

He impatiently stepped forward, shook McClory's hand and pointed to Terence. "He's right here gentlemen. The medics said my nephew has dislocated and torn his right shoulder and has lost plenty of blood. He's been in and out of consciousness for the last number of hours."

McClory nodded his head, placed a medical bag on the nearest chair and approached the table with his three men behind him. "We should be able to help."

But McClory and the others suddenly froze the moment they stepped past Jabari.

Staring coldly at them near the end of the table was the Treasure Rebels.

An unbelievable nerve-shredding silence followed.

Dr. McClory finally spoke. "Hello Maddox. Have you done much scuba diving since Egypt?"

With Jabari watching in quiet surprise, Maddox stared straight at Dr. McClory before replying.

"No. But I have been doin' quite a bit of reading."

A somewhat fearful look crossed McClory's face as he responded, "Reading...what exactly?"

Maddox replied coolly, "Your grandfather's journal."

==
(6 hours later- early evening)

John Jabari lifted a cup of cold water to Terence, who gladly took it and drank the entire 12 oz. drink in three long gulps. His thirst finally eliminated he handed the empty cup back to his uncle and closed his eyes to rest for a minute, while everyone in the dining room quietly sat around his makeshift bed which had been hastily assembled for him.

After the strange exchange between Dr. McClory and Maddox, the "Doctor" had cleaned the wound, sewn up the gash, and straightened the shoulder dislocation. Jabari hadn't asked why or how Dr. McClory knew the treasure hunters, and he didn't want to know. Now that Dr. McClory's work was finished and Terence was alert enough to speak, Jabari had asked him to explain the status of the anti-venom and helicopter.

There was complete silence except for the sound of the summer night wind rattling the branches of a nearby tree outside, and the occasional fierce crackle from the fireplace which lit up the otherwise darkened room. Terence's eyes opened and he slowly sat up, clear headed but agitated. He quickly thanked everyone for saving his life then explained in precise detail every moment of the tragedy, from the second the helicopter left the ground to the moment he had dragged himself onto the Congo River shore.

He then finished still agitated and breathless, "All the medicine is still in the cargo hold! There is excellent chance that the helicopter is still pinned to the Falls. It must be! The fishermen and their families can still be saved! You must send me back to retrieve it!"

Terence then looked up at everyone then pointed at the Treasure Rebels.

"Do these three know all about the fishermen and the anti-toxin?"

Jabari nodded his head, "Yes, I filled them in while you were being stitched up."

Jabari then looked piercingly at Dr. McClory and said sharply, "The spiders must have come from the crate you put on board the helicopter."

"I can assure you our crate was full of plants and equipment."

"Your crate looked older than I am Doctor. Why did you not transport your equipment using proper transport?"

"As I explained at the River, our boat overturned, and we lost most of our supplies. That crate was supplied to us by a farmer who said he found it years ago along the coast."

"Then perhaps there was a spider nest inside and you and your fellow botanists simply covered it with your plants and equipment."

McClory was quiet for five seconds before he simply nodded his head. "I admit that may be the sad truth."

Jabari opened his mouth to continue but was cut off by Maddox who was staring at McClory, the flames from the fireplace reflecting off his copper sunglasses.

"Did the farmer say where he found it?"

McClory smiled self-satisfied. "No, he could have found it anywhere in Africa. *Impossible for you to ever know*. I would guess somewhere along the Congo River shore."

Maddox grinned, amused at McClory's lies. "You're right. But I would have guessed he found it behind a waterfall."

McClory froze in disbelief at Maddox's statement and couldn't find any words to respond with.

Jabari turned back to his nephew and placed a large map on Terence's bed. He then shined a bright flashlight onto the map which illuminating the helicopter's route which was marked in blue ink.

"Can you remember which set of falls it crashed onto?"

"Easy, Uncle. It was right here."

Jabari looked at the spot where Terence was pointing, and his grim expression immediately turned into almost fearful despair.

"Are you certain?"

"It was that set of falls. I'm certain."

Jabari picked up the map with one hand while he had already begun dialling his cell phone for help with the other. As the number ran through he looked at the others around the bed.

"Only the military have the equipment we need."

He quickly left the dining room and walked across the hall to his office, where he spoke with over a dozen military and government officials for the next twenty minutes. He then sat in front of his computer and spent another ten minutes reading news reports from across the globe, including an interview with the billionaire Randel King from Egypt two weeks earlier.

His fax machine came to life as he expected, and fifteen pages of government papers approving visitors into the country slid out. He sat down and studied them carefully. He then heaved a long sigh, left the papers on his desk and returned to the others.

His first words were not what anyone expected, and they were directed at Maddox.

"You are Maddox Tarver, the famous person on the news, the treasure adventurer?"

"Yes sir."

"And this is Amber Monette the former NASA scientist, and Travis Jagson the heavyweight boxer from Hawaii?"

"Yes, we-"

"Do any of you have military experience?"

"No."

Jabari paused for a full three seconds before continuing, suspiciously studying Maddox and the others . "The stories in the news-media...the amazing things you and your friends have done. True or exaggerated?"

Maddox continued to reply honestly, "They are all true man."

"And you know helicopters?"

"I can fly 'em and build 'em."

"Then come with me to my office."

McClory stepped forward to protest but Jabari cut him off.

"I will be back in a few minutes to speak with you Doctor."

Maddox followed Jabari to his office, after which the businessman closed the door then sat down and offered Maddox the only chair across from him. The humanitarian didn't mince words.

"The military are only able to send one helicopter and a very small crew to pilot it. No one else. I stressed the urgency of the situation but that is the best they can do under the circumstances. I want you and your team to recover the medicine from the Chinook. You would not be working for the government or for any international humanitarian group. Only me. The medicine will be useless in you can't retrieve it before the timers run out. If you say yes I will pay you a money reward of-"

Maddox grinned, "We don't want any reward. And yes, we will do it man."

Jabari briefly smiled and leaned forward to shake hands with Maddox, convinced now that he had read the adventurer and his team correctly.

Jabari was a man of order and uprightness. He believed life was straightforward and simple. Having suffered poverty as a child and now spending his adult life helping to take care of the poor with the money he made in business, the idea of searching for treasure repulsed him. As a businessman more than a dozen treasure hunters over the years had asked him to finance their expeditions into the Congo jungle, but he always refused. Deep in his heart he felt the idea of spending his own money on the slim chance of finding treasure, instead of spending it immediately to help the poor, was somehow deeply dishonest.

Jabari understood human nature and while he could tell that some of the treasure seekers over the years had been sincere and honest, more than a few were fools at best or corrupt crooks at worst. When he learned that the government had approved a team called the Treasure Rebels to search in the jungle, he expected them to be more of the same. But once he met Maddox, Travis, and Amber in person he quickly suspected they were different. After reading about their adventures over the past two years, including what was known of their past, he was convinced they were exceptional and unlike anyone he had met before.

The only question was Maddox. His gut told him the blond twenty-something leader was of strong character, but Maddox's hipster appearance bothered Jabari.

Also despite being the teams' leader, Maddox's past was a mystery. Travis Jagson's face had graced over fifty newspapers and magazines as a world famous boxer, while Amber Monette's achievements at NASA had made her a techno-savvy superstar in the news media. But almost nothing seemed to have been written about Maddox except for a couple stories of him winning motorcycle races in the U.S. and working as a helicopter mechanic in Sweden for a year.

But when Maddox had agreed to risk his life to recover the medicine cases with no financial reward, he knew then that mystery or not, Maddox Tarver was a man worthy of trust.

Having now shaken hands in agreement, Jabari went on to explain that the helicopter would arrive at 0600 hours in the morning, and that it would be carrying a large rescue basket, cables, a rescue hoist, and hazmat suits they would wear to prevent spider bites. Maddox explained that he had rappelled from a helicopter before, and together they then outlined a rescue plan.

Ten minutes later they shook hands again and as Jabari stood to leave Maddox spoke before he opened the door.

"There's one other thing Mr. Jabari. I know he just helped your nephew, but that Dr. McClory out there ain't a real doctor."

Jabari turned away from the door. "I don't trust the man, but I watched the way he worked on Terence. I am certain he understands medicine."

"Understanding medicine and being a registered doctor are two different things."

"Dr. Fleming, one of the finest doctors in the world, confirmed Dr. McClory is legitimate, one of Greece's best physicians."

"The real Dr. McClory is probably still in Greece."

Jabari stared without uttering another word as Maddox continued.

"The man out there is Wolfgang "the Bald Artist," a professional thief who shares the same first name as his grandfather who was a Nazi. The contents of the wooden crate Wolfgang put on that helicopter don't belong to him."

Jabari paused for a moment before replying, "How could you know what was inside that crate?"

"Because that crate was what my team was looking for in the jungle."

==

(5:30 a.m. next morning - John Jabari's private estate)

Maddox, Travis, and Amber were sitting around a picnic table under one of the huge trees in front of Jabari's home. They had spent the night at a local hostel two miles away, and had returned to the businessman's home to await the arrival of the rescue helicopter at 6 a.m. Mrs. Jabari had kindly given them breakfast which they were still munching on as they discussed the situation.

"So it's straightforward. We rappel down onto the helicopter, grab the medicine cases and the old wooden crate, and after we climb into the rescue basket we're pulled back up."

Maddox finished his third drink of apple juice and nodded to Travis.

"Yes, and the whole time we're wearing reinforced hazmat suits to protect us from being bitten."

Travis tossed a roll to Jabari's happy pet bloodhound and replied seriously, "The spiders aren't the real problem. We can't know what condition the helo is in. The whole thing could topple over the falls the moment we step inside."

"I know. Jabari promised us the special equipment I asked for. That should make our job easier."

Travis tossed two more rolls to the bloodhound who barked happily as each roll came its way. He turned back to Maddox and said, "I can't believe the government is only sending one helicopter."

"He did say it was another Chinook though."

Travis then grinned, "I'm glad Jabari agreed to keep Wolfgang out of it. I'll never forget the look on his skinny creepy face last night when Jabari said he only needed us."

Maddox put his feet up on the edge of the table and stared impassively at the jungle in the distance. "He'll be waiting for us after we deliver the medicine to the village."

Travis threw two more rolls, one to Jabari's skinny bulldog and the other to his three year old boxer and replied, "Good thing then that Jabari promised us a private plane ride back to Egypt with the crate!"

At the other end of the table Amber finally spoke up as she held open old Wolfgang's notebook which she had been reading.

"Guys, we're not addressing how Wolfgang beat us to the crate."

Maddox kept looking straight forward towards the jungle and without turning replied, "Something's changed since we last saw him in the Mediterranean. I don't know how but he must have stumbled upon something critical we overlooked."

Travis said, "But I thought we were certain his grandfather only wrote one notebook...nothing else."

"I'm certain there's only one. Wolfgang never left any will or items to his only son after he died in the nineteen-fifties."

Amber looked up from reading and stated, "You're forgetting the Bounty Hunter guys. Wolfgang's only friend during and after the war. Maybe he left something behind."

Travis spit in disgust at the name and said, "That crazed mercenary left no trace of anything. We don't even know where he died."

"*If* he died."

Travis shook his head in disagreement.

"No way, the old kook would be over a hundred now."

She pushed her bright red hair out of her line of sight and replied, "He was a physical freak, if anyone could live well past the normal age expectancy it was him."

Listening to everything Maddox suddenly turned away from the jungle back to his friends and asked Amber, "Can you read page 71 from the book again? It's one of the rare moments Wolfgang talks about his partnership with him."

She turned to the right page and began, "*I've concluded my experiments in the Congo. The Bounty Hunter and I decided we needed a safe place to store my newly created medicine. The native population had been trailing us for three weeks. If they had gotten their hands on my discovery, I would never have seen it again. My friend had killed nine or more of their warriors, but that had only made them more determined to capture and eat us.*

At one point we were chased for three hours until the flesh eaters finally trapped us in a valley near the Congo River. I was certain death had finally come, and that our wives and only sons would never see us again. But my friend discovered a small cave entrance where we ran to safety. To his horror and mine the natives followed us inside. But luckily we were able to hide where they couldn't see us. They left the cave for good once a horde of bats, who oddly had two sets of fangs each, attacked them. Even my friend was savagely bitten all across his back by the horrid looking creatures. Luckily the medicinal supplies saved him, just as it had saved me from my illness.

The bats and the cannibals finally left us alone. We decided to make the cave the place to hide the medicine, and the rest of my supplies. It became our new headquarters while I made plans to return to Europe. The Bounty Hunter even set up an office in the cave, where he studied and planned to catch the man he has been chasing across the world.

His "office" was difficult to reach. But I listened to his advice to swim and follow a hairy eight legged golden spider to get there. The strange arachnid died a few weeks later due to its old age. As a safety precaution I placed the medicine behind the waterfall in the safe with the rest of my equipment. A month later we left the valley. He left nothing in his office. We will return after the war, where I will continue my search across the planet. As for the Bounty Hunter he has no interest in my goals, only in capturing his enemy...I pity that man he's hunting."

Travis grinned and looking at Maddox said, "Funny how ol' Wolfgang didn't realize the Bounty Hunter would never catch him!"

While Maddox smiled broadly at Travis' words, Amber kept looking at the notebook and said, "It's strange he never refers to the Bounty Hunter by any real name." She then scanned the rest of the pages in the yellowed leather notebook. "There's no mention he ever made it back to the Congo. After the war he visited a bunch of other exotic places, drew more maps, then on the last page he explains he's hiding the notebook in the tank for the Bounty Hunter to retrieve."

"But we know the Bounty Hunter never searched the tank," Maddox stated.

Amber sighed and swiftly closed the leather cover in frustration. "As usual, Wolfgang makes no sense. He says he's protecting the medicine from the natives, then he deliberately leaves it behind in the Congo and never returns. His drawings of the valley are incredible, but the talk of a "golden spider" sounds like a metaphor for something else."

"The word "office" could mean something else too," Travis guessed.

Amber then finished the last of her hot coffee and wondered out loud, "He said the spider died due to old age...odd."

Travis suddenly became unusually serious and turning to her said, "You know how you can tell a hairy spider is old?"

"How?"

"It's hair turns gray!"

She punched him in the arm good-naturedly as he burst out laughing.

"Enough of your jokes! Please!"

Their conversation was interrupted as the bloodhound, bulldog, and boxer suddenly bolted happily from the picnic table and up the porch steps. In a moment John Jabari and Terence appeared, arguing heavily with one another as they walked down the wooden porch and across the lawn towards them, paying no attention to the three happy dogs trotting along beside them.

Jabari looked five years older from a long sleepless night by the telephone making arrangements for the helicopter and supplies. Terence looked physically ill, and the loss of blood had weakened him. His right shoulder was covered in a huge sling that was stained with his blood in three places. Everything about his appearance said fatigue...except his eyes which burned ferociously with angry strength of will.

As they reached the Rebels they stopped arguing and Terence quickly shook each of their hands. "Thank you for saving me from the leopard! And thank you for risking your lives to retrieve the medicine! I wish to accompany you but my Uncle has forbade it, even though my home is only four miles from the crash site...and I have my own Robinson R22! I could act as point-man for-"

Jabari interrupted his nephew loudly saying, "Terence will be heading to his home. As you can see he is too weak to take part in a rescue mission."

Terence replied, "I'm not too weak to fly! Besides the doctor popped the shoulder back into place! I can simply remove the sling and-"

Jabari simply put his hand up to signal the talk was over, just as a rusted grey pickup truck drove up to the house.

"Your ride is here Terence. Get well."

Terence said goodbye to the Treasure Rebels one last time and resentfully marched to the truck which drove away with him inside moments later.

As the car disappeared out of sight Maddox said, "Your country is lucky to have a pilot as committed as him."

Jabari nodded his head, "That is why I need him to get healthy again. He would only hurt this mission and possibly make himself sicker if he took part." He then pulled out the map from the night before and handed it to Amber. "Here is the crash location. The two pilots coming have already been given precise instructions, but if there is any confusion I know you three will keep everything on course."

Ten minutes later the CH 47 Chinook transport helicopter slowly appeared through the morning fog which stretched above the jungle trees, settling down on the flat plain of grass a hundred yards in front of Jabari's estate. While the pilots stayed in the cockpit as the twin rotor blades slowed down and the engine idled, the one other crew member, a happy man in his late twenties wearing combat fatigues and a t shirt, stepped out to talk with Jabari.

As they talked Amber tucked the map into her specialized computer case while Maddox and Travis double-checked the equipment in their backpacks. She looked at them, an expression of unease across her face.

"This mission feels different. We've never done anything like it before."

"It's still the usual plan. Just now we're retrieving not only old Wolfgang's medicine in the crate but the medicine in the cases for the village too."

"Maddox I know. But...we're better as a team underwater. Helicopter rappelling isn't our specialty."

Maddox slid the backpack onto his shoulders and said, "Same plan as always. We watch each other's backs. As long as our enemies remain out of play we're fine."

Together they followed Jabari and the crew member up the ramp and into the Chinook's cargo bay. The inside of the cargo compartment was the exact same as the Chinook Terence and David had flown earlier, except now the centre of the helo contained rescue hoist and cable equipment. Bolted against one of the walls was a steel cabinet with three empty shelves, one for each of the steel medicine cases.

The crew member took ten minutes showing how the hoist worked, and explained that they would have to land after thirty minutes at a warehouse where the specialized and reinforced hazmat suits would be loaded onto the chopper.

Time to go.

Jabari warmly shook hands with each Treasure Rebel and thanked them one last time. With that he stepped back out into the humid morning as the hatchway closed behind him. Maddox and the others took seats on one side of the helicopter while the crew member sat in one of the two seats outside of the cockpit.

In moments the Chinook lifted away and headed towards the Congo River at eighty mph. After five minutes the roaring waters of Africa's greatest river appeared beneath a layer of morning fog, and the pilots set a course upriver towards the warehouse.

The ride was smooth and direct. Maddox and the others barely spoke, spending the time instead to study the rescue hoist equipment more closely. After twenty more minutes Amber looked up from her tablet.

"We should be directly over the warehouse now guys."

Just as she said the words the pilots decreased speed and began the Chinook's slow descent onto a helo pad in front of a small wooden warehouse at the edge of a swampy marsh. The landing was perfect, the engines were put to idle, and everyone began to wait except for the carefree crew member who left the helo to chat casually with the warehouse owner. The crew member spoke into his walkie talkie, and everyone on board the Chinook could hear him.

"The manager says the container hasn't arrived yet. Should be here any second. Over."

After ten minutes no sign of the hazmat suits.

Twenty minutes later the jungle road leading up to the front of the warehouse remained empty. The owner finally went back inside and placed a call while the Chinook crew member waited by the water's edge, his cheerful demeanour gone as frustration finally set in.

Inside the helo everyone had also become impatient. Travis finally said what he and his friends had been thinking for a long time.

"I hate this wait! Don't they know fifty lives are at sta-"

CRACK!

Before Maddox or Amber could respond the sound of the warehouse exploding boomed from across the empty field. The Rebels quickly rushed down the Chinook's gangway to see the tiny building covered in flames, the owner undoubtedly dead inside. The Chinook crew member lay lifeless near the water's edge shot multiple times, while a jeep carrying four men including Wolfgang screeched to a stop in front of the Chinook, assault weapons aimed at the Rebels.

With Maddox and the others forced to raise their hands in the air in surrender, Wolfgang stepped out of the jeep onto the grass, still carrying the rocket launcher he had used to destroy the warehouse moments before. He then had the Rebels hand over their knives and tranquilizer guns.

Still under gunpoint he then ordered them to walk back up into the helicopter, while his men carried the heavy fridge sized container loaded with the hazmat suits, stun guns, and other equipment onto the Chinook.

Once inside the criminals split up. One went into the cockpit to order the terrified pilots what to do next, while another went back outside to dump the jeep in the marsh. The third mercenary calmly secured the hazmat container in the centre of the hold, then took position in one of the chairs outside the cockpit. Meanwhile Wolfgang sat opposite from the Rebels, smirking arrogantly while aiming a rifle at them.

After a few moments the sound of the jeep splashing into the muddy water could be heard, and the criminal stepped back inside the Chinook, where he then hit the switch to close the cargo bay door. Simultaneously the Chinook's rotor blades increased in velocity and the aircraft lifted off.

Five minutes passed with nothing said. The only sounds were the dull humming of the blades outside and the occasional rattle of the hull as a gust of wind struck its side. Wolfgang's triumphant smirk never left his thin pale face, and after another minute he finally decided to break the silence.

He leaned forward and tapped Maddox's sunglasses while saying nastily, "How's the face?"

Maddox remained unmoved and simply said, "Still better looking than yours, man."

Wolfgang sat back in his seat surprised, laughed nervously to hide his vicious anger, and turning to Amber abruptly asked, "How's the beauty queen?"

She grinned calmly, "Still smarter than you."

Wolfgang finally looked next to Travis but was unnerved to see the last Treasure Rebel simply staring at him, unblinking, the way boxers stare down their opponents before the bell rang to start a fight.

Despite his immense height Wolfgang was still intimated by Travis's sheer physical size. While Travis was roughly half a foot shorter than Wolfgang's seven feet, he was a good thirty pounds heavier, every ounce pure muscle. Wolfgang opened his mouth to try one last taunt, but finally decided it might be a mistake and turned away from Travis' intense stare.

He called out to one of his men to bring him a laminated notepad. He flipped it open and handed it to Maddox saying, "You will carry out the mission exactly as Jabari and you planned. Here are the detailed instructions as to how the hazmat suits are meant to be worn."

Maddox handed the notebook to Amber and folding his arms calmly stretched his legs out onto the top of the container and stared at Wolfgang, his eyes hidden behind the copper coloured lenses.

"How did you beat us to the waterfall?"

Wolfgang kept the muzzle of the weapon aimed at Maddox and retorted, "What were you looking for in the Mediterranean? Did you find my grandfather's notebook there?"

"That was more than two months ago."

"What about Egypt then? Did you find my grandfather's notebook in the Nile?"

"An old journal wouldn't last five minutes in the water, let alone seventy years."

"What did you find in the river then?"

"So you **were there** on the shore watching the yacht."

Wolfgang's irritating smirk returned. "No. Someone I hired. I have contacts all over the world, especially northern Africa."

"Odd. Your nothin' like ol' grandpa. In comparison to you he was practically a loner. Only one friend."

Wolfgang stiffened and said, "My father told me about the hunter who helped grandpa. No one else on earth knows about him...You must have the notebook then."

Maddox replied poker faced and lied, "If we had the notebook we would have found the waterfall first."

Wolfgang hesitated, unsure what to think. But he seemed to buy Maddox's lie and turned his attention away from the Rebels as one of his men appeared and whispered while pointing back at the cockpit.

CONGO SPIDER FANGS

The skinny giant nodded his head in understanding then slowly stood while motioning the Treasure Rebels to do the same.

"We're about thirty minutes away from the waterfall. Open the container and suit up."

As two of Wolfgang's men undid the straps securing the container to the deck, Maddox continued speaking.

"We only want the medicine your grandfather created and the anti-toxin for the village. We're not interested in whatever else is in the old safe."

Wolfgang refused to respond, keeping the gun trained at them.

Amber spoke, "You ARE going to let us deliver the medicine to the village??"

Wolfgang continued to remain silent, but he betrayed his true intentions as the evil smirk ever so briefly appeared around the corner of his lips. Each of the Rebels saw it, and two seconds later the opportunity to escape arrived.

As Wolfgang's men opened the container Travis reached forward and threw the lid back directly into Wolfgang, smashing it into his hands and causing the assault weapon to drop onto the deck.

Chaos.

The cargo hold became a mess of brutal punches, savage kicks, and body slamming tackles. Travis finally connected with one of the thugs with his favourite right cross, and the criminal hit the deck stunned and bleeding. Maddox and Wolfgang traded punches and kicks, and when Wolfgang drew a dagger and swung Maddox grabbed his arm and rotated it until he heard the knife clatter onto the deck, followed by a sickening pop as Wolfgang's shoulder dislocated.

The hazmat suit container slid back and forth amidst the fighting, knocking Amber and her opponent to the deck. But she was back on her feet a split second faster than him, and when he stood he lifted his hands in the air in surrender as she held Wolfgang's assault rifle on him.

Wolfgang broke free of Maddox's grasp and lifted the young hero three feet off the ground with one hand, before tossing him violently against the cockpit door. But as he turned back he walked directly into Travis, who threw the hardest punch of his life. Wolfgang's nose instantly fractured, but the sociopath was only brought to his knees temporarily. With a scream he then jumped up and tackled Travis, causing both of them to crash furiously into the metal container.

The cockpit door swung open as the final thug rushed in to help his associates. But he immediately tripped over Maddox who was still slowly getting to his feet. The thug landed directly against the wall, his arm smashing into the cargo bay door lever. Instantly the large door began to open, and a storm of wind blew through the cargo hold throwing Amber and her prisoner off their feet as they were closest to the aircraft's tail. The assault weapon flew out of her hand and clattered along the deck until it slid up the opening ramp then disappeared over the open edge.

Now free for a moment inside the cockpit, the pilots immediately sealed the door and lowered the Chinook's altitude, looking for a place to land near the river. But the sudden drop in height caused havoc inside the cargo hold, and the hazmat suit container slid down the hold directly towards the open ramp...and Amber.

Travis punched Wolfgang aside and dove for the cargo bay door lever slamming it to the CLOSE position, while Maddox gave chase down the ramp.

But it was too late for both of them.

The four hundred pound container narrowly missed Wolfgang's men as it slid across the deck, instead slamming into Amber near the ramp, tossing her into open space and out of sight. A moment later it disappeared over the edge as well.

"No!" Maddox slid the final few feet as the cargo bay door began to close. All he could see before the door secured in front of him with a loud click was the dark blue waters of the Congo River forty feet below...but no sign of Amber.

He paused before turning to face everyone in the cargo hold again. Behind him he could hear Wolfgang ordering Travis to his feet, and one of the men breaking back into the cockpit where new orders were given to the pilots. In seconds he could feel the Chinook gaining altitude again.

That was Amber's only chance. That the helicopter had dropped close enough to the river to survive a fall like that. In two years the Rebels had faced death many times. But somehow those times had never felt as bleak as this. Maddox turned and raised his hands as he walked back to the bench lining the wall and sat beside Travis, who quietly sat as stunned as he was.

Maddox finally looked up at the bloodied distorted face of Wolfgang.

"We have to go back-"

"She's dead Maddox. We press forward with the mission to the helicopter."

"There is no mission without the hazmat suits for protection. The spiders kill within moments of biting."

The sick sneer reappeared as Wolfgang replied, "Then the world will be free of the Treasure Rebels."

===

Terence was having a bad day. He missed his best friend, his girlfriend hadn't called in two weeks and had probably decided to break up for good, the shoulder sling was a major annoyance, and thanks to the nearby storm of the previous day his electricity and phone was out. And his smartphone, one of the only expensive items he owned, had no battery power and with the electricity unavailable couldn't be recharged. So here he was, sitting alone in his home, resentful that his Uncle had overlooked him to help with the rescue operation.

But then the front door shook as someone outside knocked heavily four times. He slowly stood but before doing anything else he removed the sling and tossed it onto the couch in an act of minor defiance. *Enough of that*! he thought as he strolled to the door, suspecting it was one of Jabari's men who had dropped him off twenty minutes earlier.

Instead when he opened it, there standing in front of him was the good-looking redhead who had helped save him the day before. Except now her clothes were torn and covered in mud, and the beautiful smile was replaced with an expression of vicious determination.

Amber looked right at him and asked only one question.

"Terence, can you still fly your helicopter?"

PART III: SPIDER HELICOPTER

The Chinook cut through the air with a slashing roar as it approached the waterfall. The helicopter finally pushed through the heavy mist which rose above the Congo River, and the crash site finally became visible.

The original Chinook had not toppled over the waterfall's side, and was still pinned to the rocky outcropping at a 45 degree angle. The heavy waters had partially buried the rear end, but most of the fuselage and the cockpit was still discernible above the water.

The hijacked Chinook took position thirty feet above the crash site and waterfall. In the centre of the cargo hold a square hatch for rappelling was opened in the deck floor and Wolfgang's men began to ready the rescue hoist. Meanwhile Maddox and Travis waited tensely, held at gunpoint at the far end of the cargo hold.

For the last thirty minutes neither had spoken. Neither wanted to admit what they believed had been Amber's likely death. A terrible feeling of loss and despair filled their hearts. As the hoist was made ready Wolfgang's gunmen prodded them forward toward the opening in the deck floor. As they followed their captor's orders they remained quiet and their body language was slow and passive.

But their minds were working faster than they ever had before.

With Wolfgang and one of his men standing guard, another assisted Maddox and Travis into the harness. Meanwhile Wolfgang explained that the rescue basket would be lowered after them and that they were to load the old safe first, not the medicine for the village.

Travis looked through the opening in the deck floor at the damaged chopper below, and at the churning frothing water which flowed all around it. "We'll need extra cord if we're to go inside and remain attached."

Wolfgang replied coldly, "There is no extended cord. You'll have to unclip your harness before you go inside."

Maddox eyed his tranquilizer gun resting on one of the seats near the cockpit door.

"At least give us our dart guns. If we die down there you'll never get to see the safe."

"The famous Treasure Rebels don't need weapons."

Wolfgang then reached forward and pulled Maddox's sunglasses off, maliciously smiling as he put them is his shirt pocket.

"You can have them when you get back to me."

Maddox turned to look at his adversary, his fierce blue eyes surrounded by damaged and scarred tissue around his eye sockets and forehead from a shark bite months earlier.

"Oh, I'll get back to you."

The time for talk was over. Maddox and Travis took deep breaths, nodded to each other, and together rappelled down towards the damaged chopper below.

Maddox's feet touched down first, and he unclipped the harness and stepped aside to let Travis land a few moments later who did the same. Instantly both harnesses were pulled back up to the Chinook, where the rescue basket would soon be lowered down.

CONGO SPIDER FANGS

Neither Maddox nor Travis immediately moved. Instead they briefly stared at the epic sight before them. They were standing atop a crashed helicopter, which lay atop a grand waterfall as the Congo Jungle and River lay visible beneath them for hundreds of miles.

"How are we gonna get this one done? If we don't die by spider bite, Wolfgang will blow our brains out once we're back up there."

"We follow Terence's lead."

"What?"

"We jump, after we get the medicine."

"Terence was half dead when we found him! For all we know the bottom of the falls is filled with rocks. We run the risk of bashing our heads in."

"Better than a bullet through the brain from Wolfgang."

Travis spit into the water and after a moment nodded his head. "Agreed."

They slowly began walking towards the cockpit. Every step the damaged Chinook groaned, yet despite still resting partially on its side hadn't moved a foot since crashing directly into the dagger-like stone outcropping. There was a small doorway a couple feet behind the cockpit, but the force of the crash had warped the frame, along with the co-pilots door, making both impossible to open. They would have to climb inside through the damaged cockpit glass.

Slowly they reached the Chinook's nose, and Maddox leaned forward and carefully looked inside. The cockpit was knee deep in water, and the pilot's chair which was still partially visible was stained with David's blood. The pilot's side door was hanging open where Travis had jumped, and the water which poured into the Chinook's cargo hold emptied out through the open door, otherwise the helo would have simply filled completely with water. There was no sign of David, and Maddox guessed that the pilot's body had tumbled out due to gravity.

The cargo hold beyond was only barely visible due to the sunlight which streamed through the cockpit glass, and around the cracks in the hull around the stone which protruded into the centre of the compartment. The last third of the Chinook was completely shrouded in blackness.

No spiders were visible in the cockpit or in the front section of the hold. If the spiders were still inside, they were likely in the darkened tail of the aircraft.

Maddox looked up and nodded at Travis who simply replied, "Let's do this!"

Maddox turned back and crawled inside, dropping into the pool of water which came to his hips. He quickly pushed through towards the hold, holding firm to the seats to make sure there wasn't a hidden current that could suck him out through the pilot's door. Travis followed, having to completely break the cockpit glass frame so he could fit inside. After he caught up to Maddox he quickly spun around, thereby while Maddox faced towards the tail he instead always faced towards the cockpit, giving them a 360 degree view and protecting each other's backs as they moved forward.

The water wasn't freezing, and the waterline never rose above their hips. Because the Chinook had crashed partially on its side, one of the benches which lined the compartment's wall was now above their heads, and as they walked they had to carefully step around the other bench which was hidden beneath the water.

As they cautiously advanced deeper into the hold Travis said, "It's a small miracle the fuel tank wasn't hit."

"I know."

Suddenly Travis froze in alarm. "A spider just swam past my arm!"

Maddox turned and said, "Spiders can't swim. Maybe a fish was sucked inside."

BLAM!

Maddox's knee smashed into the wooden crate that contained the old safe, hidden below the water. He gritted his teeth but didn't scream at the sudden pain; instead he reached under the water and felt the top of the crate, happy to realize that the lid was off. He then reached fully inside to clutch the safe, but instead grasped four hairy and very alive spider arms which immediately pulled away from him in surprise.

This time he did scream, and he tumbled backwards into Travis causing both of them to stumble completely under the darkened water. They both broke the surface and Maddox yelled, "You were right man! Whatever they are they can survive under water! One of them's livin' right in the crate!"

A look of revulsion and horror filled Travis' face. "Then you mean the spiders...REALLY ARE SWIMMING AROUND US?!"

Without another word they both looked up and spotting the bench above their heads they grasped the steel frame and pulled themselves up completely out of the water. Hanging there they didn't say anything for a moment until Travis said the obvious.

"I really hate Wolfgang!"

Maddox instead repositioned himself directly above the crate and began swinging back and forth in the air, keeping his legs above the water. After swinging back towards the cockpit he then let his legs drop into the water as he swung back towards the tail of the chopper, using the force to kick the timeworn crate with everything he had. The rotted wood immediately cracked open and pieces of old timber quickly appeared at the water's surface.

"Yeah! Let's drag it to the cockpit and put it on the co-pilot's seat."

"But where do you think the spider went that was in the crate!"

Maddox climbed farther down the hold until his feet dangled above the safe while saying. "Just move quickly. Let's hope it's still in shock after I disturbed it."

"Shock! Spiders don't..." Travis voice trailed off and Maddox looked up.

"What is it?"

Travis nodded towards the cockpit.

Maddox looked down the hold to see three spiders crawling atop the co-pilot's seat. They were hissing and raised up on their back legs, strangely coloured and roughly four times the size of a large tarantula.

Then one jumped in the water, while the other two crawled out of the cockpit into the cargo hold, where they then scurried furiously along the dry bench towards their heads!

Maddox dropped onto the roof of the safe, which rested two feet below the water. He quickly yelled, "Hop on here!"

Travis instead yelled and swung his legs up near head level and waited for the spiders to get close. Once in range he kicked forward, the heel of his boot mangling the first arachnid and sending the second spider flying still alive into the water. He then swung around and faced Maddox.

"Let's go back to the cockpit to regroup!"

Maddox jumped up and grabbed the bench with both hands. "I agree!"

Bam! Right then one of the spiders materialized out of the shadows behind them and leaped directly onto Maddox's face. Instinctively he reached for the spider and lost his grip on the bench, plunging down into the water where he completely disappeared from view.

Travis dropped into the water to help fight but before he could do anything Maddox reappeared, the spider gone but one of its legs still stuck to the side of his face, and Maddox's hands covered in purple spider hair. Slightly stunned but still bite free he slowly stood to his full height, and then he and Travis looked at each other thinking the same thing.

They just turned and began running for the cockpit through the water as fast as possible.

But Travis didn't make it.

Another purple coloured arachnid dropped down from above directly onto Travis shoulder. He instinctively swiped it away with one hand, while another venomous spider crawled out of the water directly onto his leg…and bit straight down.

Travis grunted at the shocking pain, and reaching down he grabbed the spider and threw it against the wall with everything he had. The spider's body was pulverized at the impact as it hit a bulkhead, and remained stuck against the metallic wall cut in two.

But when Travis turned and faced his friend, his eyes and expression were full of despair.

At that moment all fear left Maddox.

He turned and dove headfirst into the water reaching the safe in one second where he then fumbled to open the door, unable to see and instead relying on touch alone. He didn't care about the threat of being bitten. His friend would be dead from the venom in moments if he didn't do something.

He felt the safe's old turn handle, and hoping that Wolfgang had already unlocked the safe in the jungle he turned it. Under water he heard the dull sombre click of the lock releasing, and he pulled the safe open as fast as possible. He reached inside, grasping papers, logbooks, pieces of machinery, and finally he felt a large vial...Wolfgang's secret medicine created decades before.

He turned and leaped out of the water, tossing the vial full of dark green bluish liquid at Travis.

"Drink one mouthful!!!"

Travis was already feeling unsteady, but he ripped the lid off and drank a quick gulp. He almost vomited, then grotesquely coughed. He then felt a terrible pain at the bite wound, and he yelled in agony. But despite the searing pain the light-headedness was already gone, and Travis reached down and pulled the floating lid out of the water and secured it back onto the vial. Perspiration was pouring down his face but his expression was one of relief as he handed the vial back to Maddox.

He knew he was going to live.

"Thanks buddy."

Maddox just smiled, "Let's just get out of here man."

As they rushed forward towards the cockpit Travis asked, "I thought the medicine would only cure Dr. Monette's disease. How did you guess it worked as an anti-venom for these spiders as well?"

Maddox replied, "When Wolfgang wrote in the journal that his medicine protected them against bites from bats, I guessed he used it as an anti-venom for the spiders in the cave as well. How else could he and the Bounty Hunter work there?"

They reached the cockpit with no sign of any more spiders.

They stepped out of the water and rested against the console and co-pilot's seat out of the water, ever vigilant in case another arachnid appeared from within the cargo hold.

Maddox continued, "The spiders look the exact same as the ones we saw kill the centipede back in the cave. I figured they were the same species, and if the medicine was used successfully all those years ago, it would still work on the same spider today."

Travis sighed and examined his leg. "If Amber were here she would be demanding that she treat the wound." He then rested his leg against the chair and stated, "It's gonna be weird giving Amber's father the medicine if she isn't there." Maddox unconsciously looked out through the cockpit glass at the Congo River far below, wondering if somehow Amber made it to shore.

"I know."

A sad moment of quiet went by as neither spoke in the cockpit. Finally Travis rested his back against the panel and pointed towards the darkened cargo hold.

"We've got old Wolfgang's medicine. Amber's dad will be fine. What about the new stuff for the village?"

"His sick grandson will just dump it all after we put it into the basket."

"Before or after he shoots us?" Travis muttered sarcastically.

"Probably after."

Suddenly one of the spiders briefly surfaced near the cockpit door, where it hissed for a moment then disappeared back under the water into the cargo hold.

Travis violently coughed twice more, finally spitting a mouthful to clear his throat.

"You okay?"

Travis grinned weakly and answered truthfully, "Good. Felt worse after some of my fights."

He then tore part of his t-shirt and after wrapping it around the bite wound bravely stepped back into the water. "Let's go get those cases and dump them over the side. Maybe one or two will be picked up by along the river by a search party. Only chance those poor fishermen in the village have."

Maddox jumped into the water and stopped his friend. "Only I should go!"

"I'm fine!"

Maddox lifted the vial up into the sunlight streaming through the glass and said, "If I get bit I've got the anti-toxin right here."

"So what? If I get bitten I'll just have another swig."

"We don't know how much is too much. We don't want to risk an overdose. You might already have had a little too much. I've never seen you look that bad before."

Travis did his best to stifle another brutal coughing attack but failed. But he didn't back down.

"I've never played it safe when other people's lives were on the line."

"You're not. We still have to jump remember?"

Travis sighed and finally assented, stepping back up onto the co-pilot seat while saying, "Well hurry up then."

Maddox tucked the vial safely into a pocket on the side of his leg, then taking a deep breath he dove back into the water and disappeared into the cargo hold, swimming just below the surface. The first ten strokes were no problem and then his fingertips brushed against the old safe. He quickly jumped out of the water and onto its roof. He then squinted at the serrated stone sticking through the chopper's hull five feet away, and the specks of sunlight which shone through a handful of tears in the hull around it.

He correctly guessed that the river water was streaming in at the bottom of the split out of sight and below the waterline. He reached up and grasped the bench, then carefully climbed until he was above the stone. Carefully he stepped down onto the portion of the stone that was above the water, vigilant to avoid the pushing surge of the water underneath it.

He then grasped a piece of the torn hull also above the waterline, and careful not to cut his hands he tried pulling it upward. The metal shrieked, the sound echoing throughout the chopper until it reached Travis in the cockpit.

The severely damaged metal only moved three inches, but it was enough as a thin ray of sunlight burst through and dimly illuminated the darkened remainder of the cargo hold. There floating half submerged against the closed cargo bay door were the three cases...and the largest spider Maddox had ever seen.

The arachnid was almost twice the size of the other spiders, including curved fangs that were nearly three inches in length. Its legs and body were so immense that it covered almost the entire surface of the case it stood on. But despite the shocking size its eight legs moved slowly and very deliberately like a tarantula, unlike the fast movements of the other spiders. As it crawled into the dim light the reason became clear: it was a completely different species of spider...and it was bright yellow. The mighty arachnid didn't seem interested in Maddox but instead gradually moved back and forth upon the cases which floated atop the water.

He then quickly wondered whether the monstrous arachnid was poisonous as well, and whether Wolfgang's medicine would hurt or help him if he drank it after getting bitten.

Nervously he stepped clear of the stone and rush of water underneath it, and guardedly approached the cases. When the massive creature slowly reached the case furthest from him, he quickly grasped the handles of the other two and turned for the cockpit. In the dim light he could see they each had digital dials which were still ticking down and read 15:24. That meant the remaining case was the one carrying the specimen. He had the medicine cases.

Each case was an engineering masterpiece, weighing only a dozen pounds despite the security features and refrigeration unit built inside. But despite the light weight each case was still exceptionally bulky, preventing Maddox from moving as fast as he wanted. His greatest concern was getting his legs bitten by one of the purple haired arachnids, and thanks to the cumbersome cases not being able to kill the spider or drink from the vial in time.

He did see two spiders scurrying above him along the bench, but neither jumped down onto his head, instead both creatures kept moving away from him towards the tail of the chopper. After the longest half minute of his life he reached the cockpit and handed the cases up to Travis who placed them against the control panel above the water.

Maddox then jumped up onto the control panel himself and said, "I think I've found a way to get into the cave office!"

"What??"

"The yellow spider!"

"WHAT!?"

Maddox didn't explain and instead he looked out through the open pilot's door and looked down at the immense drop. As Travis held the cases from sliding back into the water he said, "Ironic. Terence said he didn't throw the cases in the first place because he thought leaving them here to recover later was the better option."

He paused and sombrely looked at the digital dials ticking down before continuing, "Now we're doin' that very thing because it's the only option left." He then handed the first case to Maddox who lifted it halfway through the opening out into the open abyss.

But Maddox paused as he looked down at the tumbling waters as they poured over the edge of the waterfall with a never ending roar and disappeared beneath the opaque misty haze. He continued to pause while thinking to himself, *If only there was another way!*

Suddenly the shattered remains of the cockpit glass inside the damaged Chinook began to gently shake as sound waves from another aircraft struck the chopper. Maddox and Travis immediately looked up and out across the chasm over the falls...to see the Robinson R22 hovering two hundred feet away, with Amber grinning wildly and waving in the bubble glass cockpit towards them! Beside her Terence adjusted the controls and the tiny helicopter cut across and above the chasm towards the smashed Chinook.

Unable to contain their joy Maddox and Travis just yelled triumphantly and grabbing the two cases crawled back through the cockpit glass up outside and back onto the exposed hull of the Chinook. The R22 was hovering a mere two feet above the damaged hull, and Maddox and Travis ran towards it as fast as possible, careful not to be accidentally sliced by the R22's swirling blades.

Amber opened the co-pilot's door and Maddox and Travis quickly handed her both cases while Maddox said, "There's only ten minutes left on the timers!" She quickly replied above the roar to her friends, "There's no room in here, you have to hold onto the helo's skids!"

"Take this too!"

She looked up in surprise as Maddox handed her the old vial full of medicine. As she took it she was overwhelmed with emotion and her eyes suddenly became watery. She said simply and gratefully, "You did it Maddox... just like you promised."

But before he could even respond they were interrupted by the sound of military boots striking the outside of the chopper's exposed hull behind them. Turning they saw Wolfgang and two of his men twenty feet away unclipping their harnesses and then running towards the R22!

Maddox slammed the door while yelling, "Go!" as he and Travis each grabbed onto a skid underneath the R22's bubble cockpit. The R22 quickly lifted away...but not fast enough.

Wolfgang grabbed Maddox's leg and viciously pulled him off the R22 in one motion, while another of his men threw a knife directly into Travis right leg, just below the bite wound. With a grunt of savage pain Travis dropped onto the hull near Maddox as the two mercenary thugs closed in on him.

In the R22 now ten feet above them, Terence and Amber were horrified as they watched the carnage below. "Wolfgang's going to kill them!"

Terence was hardly listening, and instead took action. He manipulated the controls and the Robinson burst forward past Travis and Maddox, and then dropping a few feet continued forward until the glass bubble cockpit smashed directly into the two mercenaries. Both criminals were savagely pushed in opposite directions. One fell partway into the roaring water while still holding onto the Chinook with one hand, while the other disappeared over the edge of the waterfall and fell the sixty feet screaming until he fatally hit one of the hidden stones at the bottom with a bloody crack.

Behind the R22, Maddox and Wolfgang fought each other with everything they had, and when Wolfgang quickly pulled out a handgun Maddox expertly grabbed and spun Wolfgang's arm...which sent the gun tumbling into the water. Wolfgang responded by grabbing his hated rival and throwing him madly over his shoulders.

Maddox landed hard onto the steel hull, but he quickly rolled and brought Wolfgang crashing down with a vicious and unexpected kick. He then stood and looked up at the Robinson hovering a dozen feet in the air, then at the lone mercenary who had already climbed out of the swirling black water. He knew the village was almost out of time and that the R22 couldn't wait any longer.

So he signalled Amber and Terence to leave.

Amber looked down at the digital dials inside the small chopper. Barely 8 min. left. She wanted to stay, but she knew he was right. Sombrely she nodded and the Robinson turned away and continued across the Congo River for the village. Terence knew every second counted, and the little helicopter was quickly flying well over 100 mph.

The mercenary ran towards Travis who hurriedly pulled the knife out of his leg before trying to climb to his feet. But before he could swing the blade the thug had kicked the weapon out of his hand, and then punched him back to his knees. Travis struggled to regain his balance while he tried to block every punch and kick. He wouldn't admit it, but thanks to his wounds he had never felt weaker in any fight before in his life.

Despite the pain he climbed back to his feet and tried a kick of his own with his good leg, but the mercenary quickly blocked it and spun him to the side before delivering a roundhouse kick that landed directly into his stomach. He stumbled back, the pain so intense he couldn't even yell.

But then the mercenary made his mistake. Seeing Travis stumble back in agony, he rushed as close as he could and tried to land a direct kick down onto Travis' wounded leg. But in doing so the thug left himself wide open, and despite the agony he felt Travis still reacted perfectly, throwing an intense left uppercut that connected directly into the bottom of the mercenary's jaw. The thug staggered backward, still on his feet. But Travis saw the strange expression in his eyes and knew he was unconscious before he finally collapsed.

Ten feet away Maddox and Wolfgang fought furiously. Every punch and kick carried with it their anger of the last two years of combat, rivalry, and trying to outrace the other to find the safe. Maddox knew the skinny murderer had finally lost all self-control, and that now sensing the Treasure Rebels were about to outwit him for the final time, had given up on the safe and now only wanted to kill them.

After they each landed a couple of punches and kicks, Wolfgang ominously drew a long dagger from behind his back...his eyes finally showing the hateful insanity that was behind them.

Maddox wasn't intimidated.

He easily dodged two of Wolfgang's hateful swipes with the knife, then he jumped forward and tackled Wolfgang directly, slamming the seven foot criminal hard onto the helicopter's hull, so hard that the chopper actually shook with the impact. The dagger soared out of Wolfgang's hand and tumbled across the deck, along with Maddox's sunglasses which flew out of the emaciated murderer's shirt pocket.

The dagger disappeared over the side and plopped into the water, but Maddox slid across the hull and grabbed the copper shades with one hand just before they reached the edge.

Triumphantly he stood and put the sunglasses back on over his facial wounds, nodding to Travis who simply gave him the thumbs up while grinning faintly.

Both Wolfgang and his hired mercenary lay unconscious.

Travis spit over the side into the water and said in a hoarse voice, "What about the last one up there holding the pilots hostage?"

Maddox looked up at the Chinook hovering thirty feet above them.

"You stay and guard these two freaks."

==

As the R22 raced across the Congo towards the village, Amber continued to try the radio for help with no success. Only static filled her headset, no matter the frequency or channel she chose. Terence apologized and said, "I'm sorry, the village doctor will have a radio we can use when we land. I know because my Uncle was talking to him last night when he was making plans for the rescue mission. Perhaps he has already called Jabari to ask why the medicine hasn't arrived."

Amber frowned and replied, "Even if they have talked Jabari doesn't know about the hijacking yet."

She then looked at the cases to see where the timers stood. 4:00 min. to go.

She turned back to the radio and was actually a little glad for its distraction. Amber enjoyed almost all aspects of aviation, but even though she could fly herself she despised tiny helicopters like the R22. She hated the sensation of feeling only a glass bubble separated her from the open sky, and that the entire R22 felt no bigger than a small car. She much preferred flying in airplanes, jets, or much larger helicopters.

But she kept her feelings to herself, not wanting Terence to laugh at her and think she was weak, especially after he had explained to her earlier how he loved the feeling of freedom the R22 provided.

Terence also kept his own concerns to himself so Amber wouldn't think he was weak. But his doubts had nothing to do with the R22 but with himself.

Terence now realized that his shoulder injury was more severe than he originally thought. The anger at his Uncle followed by the adrenaline rush of getting the chance to still help was finally wearing away, and now the pain in his arm was taking over. He also was beginning to feel lightheaded. He hadn't taken any pain killers, knowing if he did so he couldn't fly due to the drowsiness they caused.

So why was he feeling so weak??

The pain temporarily went away as he suddenly saw dozens of small wooden houses clumped together a couple hundred yards downriver to their right lining a small wooden pier. He quickly pointed at it and exclaimed happily, "There it is Miss Redhead!"

She heaved a sigh of relief and looked at the cases as Terence guided the R22 down towards the small dock at the edge of the village.

2:00 min. to go.

"You're a marvellous pilot Terence."

But he didn't respond.

Instead Terence slowly slumped forward unconscious directly onto the cyclic control, and the R22 plummeted while spinning madly towards the dock!

Amber screamed and reaching forward pulled Terence back into his seat and shook him, but the young pilot was completely unresponsive. As the ground came spinning upwards towards the glass cockpit she immediately switched control from Terence's side to hers, giving her control of the R22's cyclic, pedals, collective, and other instruments.

At fifty feet above ground she managed to pull the R22 up before it smashed into the wooden docks, and she dramatically reduced the R22's speed. But she wasn't able to completely stop the wild spinning, and despite her best efforts she was never able to regain complete control...and the helo flew over the village before it suddenly dipped down and plunged directly into the top of a large tree fifteen feet above the ground. The interior of the cockpit shook violently, and the glass bubble cracked and broke in a thousand different places while the rotor blades continued to slice and chop through the branches.

Amber shook her head and immediately felt blood trickle down the side of her face, but she kept her composure and realizing that the R22's tail and skids were stuck in the tree's immense branches she reached forward and shut down the power. The rotors came to a stop, and she looked at Terence who still sat completely still, but was breathing.

She then turned to open her cockpit door, and realized it had been torn clear of the hinges...and that the medicine cases were nowhere to be seen. She looked frantically around until she spotted them resting fifty feet away at the base of another tree...bent and twisted.

She then heard voices and looking down saw five men from the village calling up to her, while two old ATV's idled beside them. She called back that the pilot was hurt, and they quickly responded in moments by placing ladders along each side of the damaged fuselage of the Robinson R22. In moments the men were trying to talk to Terence and he very slowly began to wake and respond.

Seeing that Travis was taken care of she then stepped out onto the branches and grasped a steel rung of a ladder, then after securing her feet on a rung below she climbed down. Once on the ground she was quickly surrounded by some of the men who were pointing to her head then waving towards the village yelling, "DOCTOR! You need DOCTOR!"

She ignored them and rushing across the sand covered grass she scooped up one of the damaged medicine cases and looked at the dial. It was frozen at 0:45 seconds. The case also felt different, and she suspected the refrigeration unit inside had finally quit. She then scooped up the other one which was so badly smashed the digital dial was broken and unreadable.

She turned to the men and said, "Now take me to the Doctor!!!"

Three minutes later one of the ATV's with Amber aboard braked in a cloud of dust in front of a small modest one story home. She quickly knocked but no one answered. She pounded harder against the plywood door and called out for help.

"I am the doctor here."

She turned at the voice and saw an elderly Congolese man wearing a lab coat peer out from behind a door directly across from her. Written in plain English above the doorway was one word: *Hospital*.

She yelled across to him while holding up the cases, "Hurry! I have the medicine!" The old man immediately ran towards her as fast as his old legs would allow, and as the hospital door slowly closed behind him she could briefly see inside at the faint outline of dozens of people lying in medical beds.

Amber handed the two cases to the elderly man who happily took them and walked up into his home, followed by Amber and the fisherman who had driven the ATV. Once inside the Doctor placed them both atop his kitchen table and after examining the smashed frames he said, "Stand back for safety...not sure if components or refrigeration units inside are still intact." After they obeyed he quickly typed a number into the keypad in each case, which was followed by a loud click and a whooshing sound as the lids popped open a couple centimetres.

Slowly the elderly man completely lifted the lids...to reveal the orange vials were secure and intact in each case. He then picked up a vial carefully from each case and smiled, "Still very cold!"

He then reached forward and with tears of gratitude streaming down his face he warmly shook her hand and said, "You have saved our village young woman!"

He then pointed to her head and exclaimed, "Nasty, nasty cut! I will take care of that so-"

She cut him off and pointed to an old CB radio which sat on another table beside the front door.

"I need first to call Mr. Jabari!"

===

Maddox climbed the thirty feet up the cable towards the Chinook roaring above the crash site. With no-one operating the winch he had to climb under his own power, but he made it to the opening in less than thirty seconds.

He correctly guessed the remaining mercenary had stayed in the cockpit, not risking the pilots being left alone. But he also hesitated before climbing back up into the cargo hold, suspecting that Wolfgang's last man had also likely spotted him climbing up, and would be waiting. He hesitated at the opening, and then after grasping the edge with both hands he pulled himself up through and then forward, rolling clear of the opening in one smooth and incredibly fast move. The moment he appeared the thug opened fire from the open cockpit door, and a series of wild, yellow sparks scattered across the cargo hold.

But none of the bullets came close to Maddox, who came to a rolling stop behind the empty steel cabinet. He looked around for a weapon but the only ones nearby were assault rifles. He wasn't going to fire one of them at the thug and risk destroying the Chinook's control panel or kill the pilots in the cockpit.

Then one of the pilots decided to fight back. With the mercenary's back turned he signalled the other pilot who nodded his head in understanding. As the mercenary began to taunt Maddox to come out, the brave pilot attacked him savagely from behind.

The pilot fought ferociously, even landing a hard punch directly into the criminal's ribcage, and pinning the mercenaries' hand in an attempt to get him to drop the weapon. But the gun instead went off three times straight into the control panel, and the Chinook immediately began to sputter and shake in response. The other pilot did everything in his power to keep control, but in vain.

The mercenary was a trained fighter, and after finally grabbing the pilot by the throat he threw him easily to the floor. The mercenary was also a killer, and he aimed the handgun at the pilot in rage and began to pull the trigger.

CLICK-CLICK.

He froze at the sound of one of the assault rifles being loaded. He turned to see Maddox smiling and standing behind him in the cargo hold, pushing the muzzle of the rifle against his head. The mercenary dropped the gun and the pilot happily got back to his feet and began helping his co-pilot regain control of the helicopter. Down below Travis watched in agony as the helo continued to lose altitude...and spin directly towards the edge of the waterfall.

But the Chinook suddenly stopped dropping, and the helicopter regained its normal altitude and turned back until it was once again directly over Travis below. Inside the cockpit both pilots continued to wrestle feverously with the controls, while Maddox and the mercenary watched from behind, the criminal no longer interested in fighting and instead only wanting not to drop over the falls.

The main pilot finally looked up, his face full of perspiration and his hands trembling with the extreme stress as the Chinook began shaking violently. "She's dying. We can only keep her up for a few more moments."

Maddox suddenly handed the rifle to the other pilot who had fought back, and pointed to the opening in the cargo hold deck behind him. "All of you rappel down to the chopper below…I'll keep her steady."

The co-pilot took the rifle uneasily, "You know how to fly?"

Maddox didn't respond, instead he simply sat straight down in the co-pilot's chair and instantly took control of the stick, and began monitoring and adjusting the dials and switches to maintain power. The shaking suddenly stopped, and the Chinook temporarily straightened out. The pilots paused for a moment and looked at one another in surprise, then after quickly thanking Maddox they ran out of the cockpit towards the opening, holding the rifle on the mercenary who happily followed their orders.

In twenty seconds all three men had clipped harnesses to the line and with Travis's help below safely slid the thirty feet down to the damaged chopper. After unclipping the last pilot Travis looked up expectantly at the Chinook as smoke began to curl out of its sides while the engine shrieked in horrible protest.

But no sign of his friend.

Inside the Chinook Maddox tried the auto-pilot system but it was unresponsive. He tried every tactic he knew to keep the chopper stable for fifteen seconds so he could bail through the opening. But he knew the second he let go of the controls the chopper would pitch forward away from Travis and everyone else below, and fly towards the precipice of the waterfall instead.

Suddenly the chopper began shaking even more violently, and the entire aircraft immediately spun to the left then dropped until it was just thirty-six inches above the churning water, and only a dozen feet from the precipice. Maddox held on with everything he had, barely keeping the helicopter above the waterline. He looked out through the cockpit glass at Travis a hundred feet away to his right as the roaring river water splashed against the cockpit glass with every high wave.

He tried gaining altitude but the chopper wouldn't respond.

In growing alarm he knew the Chinook would drop into the water in moments, and he would be carried over the waterfall's edge into the abyss. And even if he could climb out in time, with the current he would never be able to swim the hundred feet across to Travis before being sucked over.

He had only one option.

He immediately shifted the controls and spun the Chinook 180 degrees, till it was facing away from the falls. He then tried to increase the engine's power and the Chinook weakly responded, flying barely above the water and slowly for two hundred feet. He then adjusted the controls and the Chinook spun 180 degrees again, so the nose was now facing towards the waterfall while the tail was facing away from it. He then reached up and pushed the button to open the cargo bay door just as the Chinook finally died and dropped into the swirling black water, where it was quickly pulled towards the falls by the current.

He cut the power and as the blades were slowing down he jumped up from the seat and entered the cargo hold, grabbing Amber's tablet computer and his loaded tranquilizer gun as he made his way towards the helicopter's tail and the opening cargo bay door.

The cargo hold began to swiftly fill with water through the opening in the deck floor and also through the widening cargo bay door. For the second time in less than an hour, Maddox was running through the inside of a helicopter knee deep in water. As he reached the end a loud screech filled the hold as the chopper's mechanical systems continued to shut down, and the cargo bay door screeched to a stop.

He paused and took stock. The cargo bay door had only opened four feet before grinding to a halt. He looked back and thought of swimming through the opening in the deck floor and swim underneath the Chinook, but then wondered whether the current would be too strong for him to resurface.

He made his decision. He continued running forward, leaped up and grabbed the steel of the cargo bay door and quickly pulled himself up and rolled through the opening before dropping headfirst into the bubbling river water.

He was able to reach the surface in a couple seconds but as he spit out the water and looked up he realized with horror that the current was moving much faster than he expected. The Chinook was already thirty feet ahead of him, and in an almost surreal moment as if time had suddenly slowed, he watched as the helicopter reached the precipice then tumble over the falls, spinning as it disappeared over the edge. In two seconds the Chinook hit the boulders below and exploded, sending a fireball eighty feet into the blue sky, giving the brief impression that a wall of fire lay beyond the waterfall's edge.

He then realized that he was being carried away from Travis and the damaged chopper stuck on the rocky outcropping to his right, and that he would be pushed over the falls in a matter of moments. He was only ten feet away from Travis, but it seemed like ten thousand. He swam as fast as he could to close the gap, while Travis leaned out of the water as far as he could to grab him.

But the gap *was* too far.

As the precipice grew closer Maddox realized he simply couldn't swim close enough in time to reach Travis' outstretched hand.

But Travis could still close the distance. With one last act he climbed up and onto the damaged rotor shaft and after curling his foot around it he climbed partway out onto one of the blades and stretching his arm grabbed his friend by the shoulder three feet from the waterfall's edge. With a yell he lifted Maddox with the one arm, the muscles and tendons literally shaking from the strain, and he dropped his friend onto the chopper's exposed tail section after which Maddox quickly climbed forward to join the others to safety.

Seeing that Wolfgang and his men were being guarded by the two pilots, Maddox then simply collapsed onto the exposed hull of the chopper and laughed, utterly exhausted. Travis climbed back down and limped towards his friend, drained of all energy and leaving behind a tiny trail of blood from his leg wounds.

He sat down beside Maddox and said simply while smiling tiredly, "I need home. I need Hawaii. And I need it right now!"

==================================----------------

For the next two hours everyone sat quietly atop the smashed chopper until in the distance they spotted a Robinson R44 approach with Amber smiling in the co-pilot's seat with one of Jabari's men piloting the aircraft. The helo hovered a couple feet in the air, and Amber swung open her door and climbed down to see her friends.

All three hugged each other at the same time. They pulled apart and Amber explained, "Jabari is sending more help. A rescue chopper should arrive any minute to pick up everyone who can't fly back with me."

'Did you get the medicine delivered in time?"

She smiled even more and answered Travis, "YES!! The medicine is still being administered as we speak."

Travis looked at the pilot in the larger R44 and inquired, "Where's Terence?"

"He was worse for wear than he thought. He actually passed out from loss of blood. But the doctor there says he'll be okay. The bigger R44 belongs to one of Jabrai's friends who owed him a favour."

Maddox then asked, "The R22 is still at the village then?"

She smiled and pointed to the stitches barely visible along the top of her red hairline "We had a rough landing."

She then looked at everyone aboard and asked the obvious. "Where's the other Chinook?"

"At the bottom of the falls."

All three Treasure Rebels then burst out laughing, unbelievably thrilled and amazed they were all still alive.

A moment passed and then Maddox pointed at the R44. "You should take Travis back to get his wounds looked at, the rest of us can wait for the rescue chopper."

"Why can't you come too?"

Maddox instead just replied, "Can I borrow the medicine for a moment? I'll give it back before you take off."

Puzzled she handed the old vial to him after which he turned and walked back towards the chopper's damaged cockpit.

Travis' eyes bulged in surprise and he yelled, "What are you doing!! All three of us have cheated death today! Forget the safe!"

Maddox just grinned, pulled the tranquilizer gun out of the holster and said, "I'm not interested in the safe!" And with that he then disappeared back inside the spider filled helicopter.

EPILOGUE

(One month later – Congo Jungle Valley – 10 miles from John Jabari's home)

The gentle bubbling waters of the ravine and the almost serene sound of the waterfall were suddenly drowned out by the sound of helicopters approaching. Two Robinson R44 choppers, one painted blue the other red, sliced through the sky and entered the clearing where they slowly landed beside the ravine.

The engines were shut down, the cockpit doors were opened, and the Treasure Rebels stepped back into the valley where they had discovered the cave a month earlier. John Jabari and Terence also joined them from the other chopper, and all five men and woman stood and looked in awe at the waterfall which fed the ravine.

After a couple seconds Jabari finally spoke, handing Maddox a tan coloured backpack.

"It's in here. I have to tell you Mr. Tarver that it scared more than a few people who saw it."

Maddox put the backpack on and replied, "Thanks for keeping it for the last month until we could come back to Africa."

"You three certainly deserved the break and time to heal!"

Jabari then shook each of their hands and thanked them for the tenth time for saving the village.

He then continued, "I want you three to know that the criminal Wolfgang and his men have been deported and are facing charges in twenty different countries. Thanks also to you they will never kill again or be free."

Travis replied, "No one's happier than me to know that sick skinny rat won't be following us anymore!"

Jabari continued, "I also want you to know that the contents of the safe will be delivered to you once it is safely extracted from the helicopter. As of right now the government is still trying to figure out what to with the Chinook...it still sits pinned against the falls."

He then noticed the small vials of medicine around each of their necks and said to Amber, "I presume that is the medicine from the safe...I heard your father needed it?"

She smiled, "He would have died in a matter of days without it. Now he can go back to his work saving the lives of others."

"So you didn't come to the Congo for treasure!"

"That's right Mr. Jabari."

He genuinely laughed at the admission and replied wholeheartedly, "Medicine to save the life of a loved one is certainly better than any treasure!"

With his arm in a sling Terence stepped forward and thanked them as well.

"You guys are heroes!"

Maddox responded, "Thanks for your help too, but don't forget we didn't recover all the cases."

Terence shook his head and said, "No problem! There was enough medicine in the two cases for every person bitten by the reptiles. And Dr. Fleming has informed my Uncle here that a farmer in the north just captured another one and is having it shipped here. In twenty four hours Dr. Fleming will be able to continue studying the new species!" He then shook Maddox and Travis' hand, then insisted on a hug for Amber for saving his life. Off to the side Maddox and Travis couldn't keep a straight face as she reluctantly agreed.

John and Terence then waved goodbye one final time and climbed back inside the chopper. After a minute the R44 lifted off and headed back towards the businessman's estate.

The valley became quiet again, and Maddox led the way back into the cave.

As they walked carefully through the twisting passageway Maddox and Travis couldn't help but kid Amber about Terence.

"You know I never took you for the hugging type."

"Stop it!"

Travis joined in and laughed, "Wait till he finds out you have a fiancé'!"

"Enough!"

They reached the main cave where the shell-like remains of the monster centipede were barely visible amongst the dirt and dust, and there were no spiders to be seen. To be safe Travis pulled out a tranquilizer gun and briefly swept the cave with his flashlight.

Maddox took off the backpack and walked towards the base of the falls before stopping at the edge of the small ravine below it. He set the backpack down and unzipped it, and while Travis and Amber watched apprehensively he pulled out a large container twice the size of a shoebox.

Suddenly the box came to life and began to quiver in his hands. Still completely calm Maddox held on and was handed a mask and snorkel from Amber. He set the box down, put the mask and snorkel on, then with a big grin he carefully undid a special seal around the box and opened one of its edges before quickly dumping it forward in one smooth motion.

The enormous yellow spider from the helicopter fell out and plopped into the ravine, where it slowly began to swim away.

Maddox immediately dove in and followed it.

Under the water visibility was difficult but not impossible. Because the spider was almost the size of a small cat and moved through the water slowly, it wasn't too hard for Maddox not to lose sight of it. After half a minute of swimming the spider suddenly turned to the right away from the cave wall that led to the outside, and instead followed a hidden and darker tunnel further into the cave.

Maddox followed but suddenly lost sight of the arachnid. He quickly picked up speed but immediately felt his outstretched hands collide with a rocky wall. A dead end.

He quickly felt in the dark and looked around but couldn't see anything. Then his hand broke free of the water and he realized it was only a dead end under the water. He reached up, felt dirt and rocks, and pulled himself out.

To reveal a hidden underground cave roughly eight hundred square feet in width, and extending a hundred feet up to the open jungle above, where large shafts of sunlight streamed down between the tree limbs. Off to the side the yellow spider struggled to crawl across the sand until it reached a crevice in the far wall, climbed inside and disappeared.

He slowly walked across the sand to see a rickety table littered with newspapers from the 1950's, and a large bulletin board pinned with handwritten papers, maps, drawings of animals, diagrams of engines...and one picture.

Maddox stepped forward and looked at the black and white photo in astonishment. It showed the face of a man who stared back at the camera with confidence and defiance. Maddox knew who the man was, and that it was the only picture ever taken of him. Above the photo was a world map, with over thirty countries circled. Beside certain places handwritten notes had been stuck to the map. But one place stood out from the rest in South America, circled in now faded red ink with the words, "GOT YOU NOW!" written beside it, along with the date and year.

Maddox turned back to the photo, and almost in awe he took the picture down, folded it carefully and placed it in a waterproof pocket. Just then Travis and Amber broke the surface and stepped up into the cave to join him.

Travis and Amber took off their illuminated dive goggles and walked up to Maddox while taking everything in.

"We missed you taking that right turn! Luckily our goggle lights bailed us out!"

"So this was the Bounty Hunter's office!"

"Where's the yellow spider!?"

"It doesn't matter Travis, Dr. Fleming said its venom is harmless to humans despite the large fangs."

"You're forgetting I know what it feels like to be bitten by excessively large spider fangs!"

As they talked back and forth Maddox didn't join in, instead he noticed the last item in the cave beside the desk and bulletin board...a beautiful Harley 1943 WLC motorcycle, painted green and resting under a beam of light a dozen feet away from the desk.

He bent down and examined it, wondering what amazing adventures it had been a part of.

Travis looked at the old bike respectfully and said, "The Bounty Hunter was a kook, but he sure understood how to take care of a motorcycle."

Without looking up Maddox replied, "It didn't belong to him."

Travis looked down at Maddox perplexed, "What? Who else could it have belonged to? His buddy Wolfgang?"

Behind them Amber lifted her tablet sized computer and used it as a camera to take pictures of everything on the bulletin board and desk.

She overheard Travis and said, "I bet it belonged to the man he was hunting!"

Travis turned to Maddox who simply nodded yes.

Travis beamed, "He's even cooler than you said he was!"

They spent ten more minutes examining the Bounty Hunter's old haunt, until Amber's satellite phone suddenly beeped. She picked it up then spoke for half a minute before ending the call.

"That was Jabari. Our flight has been bumped up and leaves in a few hours. He apologized but there's nothing he can do. We have to go if we're going to catch it."

Maddox nodded his head but looked lost in thought.

"Jabari also said we can return whenever we want."

Maddox's smile returned and together he and his two friends slipped back into the water. But Maddox took one last look at the old cave, then at the crevice in the wall where the spider had vanished. Finally ready he dove in and headed back towards the helicopter in the valley.

=======================================

Two hours later the red Robinson R44 set down quietly on the tarmac in one of the Congo's smaller airports.

Immediately they sensed something was wrong.

The large waiting room should have been filled with people impatient to board their plane for Egypt. Instead they could see through the windows that the waiting room and office only contained a few bored looking members of the ground crew and staff. And while there were two small planes at the far side of the airport being refuelled, the rest of the tarmac was bare, with no sign of any large passenger plane.

"They must have left without us!"

Amber agreed with Travis and began dialling Jabari's number.

As she did so a member of the ground crew left the office and ran up to the R44 to speak with Maddox.

"Can I help you?"

"Where is the passenger plane headed for Egypt man? It's supposed to take off in ten minutes."

The ground crew worker shook his head and replied, "It was ordered to leave five minutes ago…to make way for the incoming Airbus."

Maddox opened his mouth to respond but stopped as he spotted the multimillion Airbus H155 airplane suddenly appear on the horizon and head for the runway.

Amber leaned forward and asked the man, "The pilot would have known three important passengers hadn't yet boarded. Why would a small plane like the airbus be given special treatment over a passenger plane full of people?"

The crewman shrugged his shoulders and replied sincerely, "Because we were told some celebrities called the Treasure Rebels were to board the airbus."

The crewman jumped back down and headed back to the office as Maddox and the others sat still in quiet shock. Amber's call suddenly went through and John Jabari's voice could be heard through the speaker. She quickly explained the situation and he replied, "I never gave any order! I'll call the airport myself this minute to sort out the error."

She thanked him and ended the call as the Airbus, painted silver with blue streaks, landed onto the tarmac and taxied to a stop at the end of the runway. But the small passenger plane suddenly came to life again, moving away from the office and instead slowly rolling to a stop twenty feet in front of the Robinson R44.

The air-stairs were lowered, and two people they had never seen before stepped down and walked towards the helicopter. Carefully, the Treasure Rebels exited the chopper and walked across the tarmac to meet them, curious and uneasy at the same time.

The first stranger was a six foot tall man roughly forty years of age, who had extremely short almost shaved dyed brown hair, and was dressed in a tuxedo that was almost tearing at his arms due to his large biceps.

Beside him was a woman almost a decade younger, dressed in a long purple evening gown with her blond hair tied back in a ponytail. As they drew closer both Maddox and Travis were temporarily stunned at her beauty...until they saw her eyes.

Emotionless, cold, and empty of any charisma, her eyes were even more sinister looking than Wolfgang's.

The mysterious man addressed them first.

"Maddox Tarver. Travis Jagson. Amber Monette. My sister and I request your help in locating something important...something that belonged to our grandfather."

Travis disliked the man immediately and rumbled back, "And who was he?"

"The Bounty Hunter."

Travis and Amber couldn't speak and simply stood stunned, while Maddox simply smiled back at the mysterious strangers, the surprised expression in his eyes hidden beneath the sunglasses.

Suddenly behind them a black Hummer drove onto the tarmac and rolled to a stop, after which four gunmen stepped out and circled them.

The mysterious man then gestured for the Treasure Rebels to climb up into the Airbus.

"We'll tell you where were heading once we're all seated."

Under gunpoint they resentfully followed orders and climbed up into the small passenger plane, where two more gunmen inside ordered them to sit down in the plush passenger seats. A minute later the mysterious man and woman entered the cabin and sat opposite them as the Airbus began to pull away down the tarmac for take-off.

The woman leered at them and said, "I understand how uncomfortable you three must be right now...you will have to get used to following my brother's orders and mine."

Travis and Amber refused to respond and only stared back with rage. But Maddox lifted his muddy boots and dropped them onto the table in front of his captors, grinning and relaxed.

The man in the tuxedo tried to ignore Maddox and said, "I suppose you three want to know where we're headed."

"The Amazon River."

The man looked at Maddox in surprise and paused unsure of what to say next. Deep down he sensed that somehow Maddox knew far more than he did, and that the spikey haired adventurer had a significant advantage over him.

"How...how...did you know that?"

Maddox simply thought back to the bulletin board in the cave and smiled back.

"A little spider told me."

Don't miss out!

Visit the website below and you can sign up to receive emails whenever Gerard Doris publishes a new book. There's no charge and no obligation.

https://books2read.com/r/B-A-WRCD-OGZL

BOOKS 2 READ

Connecting independent readers to independent writers.

Did you love *Congo Spider Fangs*? Then you should read *Amazon Swamp Victory*[1] by Gerard Doris!

[2]

The Treasure Rebels are taken to the Amazon Rainforest and forced to search for a priceless dive helmet hidden in the murky depths of a jungle swamp. A swamp that contains electric eels, other incredible dangers, and the rusted underwater ruins of a destroyed steamboat.

With their lives on the line, the Rebels set out to not only outwit their enemies and locate the helmet, but to find the answer to a legendary mystery more thrilling than any treasure hunt. "Amazon Swamp Victory" is the third adventure in the

---

1. https://books2read.com/u/3GYxaK

2. https://books2read.com/u/3GYxaK

Treasure Rebels novella series, and directly follows the wild events of "Congo Spider Fangs."

Read more at https://www.adventurefictionforever.com.

Also by Gerard Doris

Treasure Rebels
Nile River Scorpion
Congo Spider Fangs
Amazon Swamp Victory
India Yeti Pirates
Greek Gladiator Sharks

Standalone
Wrath of the Renegades

Watch for more at https://www.adventurefictionforever.com.

About the Author

Thanks for reading! I write adventure fiction that features treasure hunters, pirates, and renegades. I'm also a fan of NFL football, westerns, classic action movies, and anything that promotes genuine adventure. For some fun updates on my writing projects, you can follow me on Twitter at https://twitter.com/gerard_advfict

Read more at https://www.adventurefictionforever.com.

Milton Keynes UK
Ingram Content Group UK Ltd.
UKHW040719161023
430697UK00001B/32